Revenge

King Crawley controlled a vast underworld empire, but he was powerless over the disease racing through his body. Time was running out for the King.

He'd lost his wife, his daughter and his son. Hatred was all King Crawley had left. Hatred of Judge Raferty, who in his weakened state would be dealt a final, mortal blow.

Asia Raferty was the apple of her father's eye, the child closest to his heart. King Crawley had no time for finesse and no need to cover his tracks as he planned the climax of his vendetta.

Before he left this world, King Crawley would enjoy a last, sweet victory—the death of love.

Asia Raferty is King Crawley's final victim. In case you've missed Book One #161 *Pushed to the Limit* (May 1991) and Book Two #163 *Squaring Accounts* (June 1991) in the QUID PRO QUO series, you can still order both through the Harlequin Reader Service.

Dear Reader,

The idea for writing a series of connected mysteries has intrigued me for years. My opportunity and greatest challenge came with the idea for QUID PRO QUO. I hope you'll enjoy the final book in the series as you travel with Asia and Dominic on their journey in finding a solution to King Crawley's vendetta.

In case you've missed the first and second books in the series, you can still order May #161 *Pushed to the Limit* and June #163 *Squaring Accounts*.

Patricia Rosemoor

No Holds Barred

Patricia Rosemoor

Harlequin Books

TORONTO • NEW YORK • LONDON
AMSTERDAM • PARIS • SYDNEY • HAMBURG
STOCKHOLM • ATHENS • TOKYO • MILAN

To my husband, Edward Majeski,
for finding the facts—and holding my hand—
when I'm desperate.

Harlequin Intrigue edition published July 1991

ISBN 0-373-22165-4

NO HOLDS BARRED

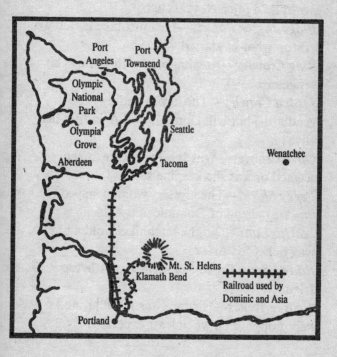

Port
Angeles

Port
Townsend

Olympic
National
Park

Olympia
Grove

Seattle

Aberdeen

Tacoma

Wenatchee

Mt. St. Helens
Klamath Bend

┿┿┿┿┿┿┿┿┿┿┿┿
Railroad used by
Dominic and Asia

Portland

CAST OF CHARACTERS

Asia Raferty—Caught in a race for her own life, she joins forces with the enemy.

Dominic Crawley—Guilt makes him face a world he'd rejected years ago.

Judge Jasper Raferty—He must take action to stop what he started.

King Crawley—At what price will he have his vengeance?

Jessica Crawley—The key to ending the vendetta—but will Dominic and Asia find her alive?

Olive Crawley—Was she as delicate as she seemed or was she keeping secrets?

Peggy Shield—The mystery woman stayed one step ahead of Dominic and Asia.

Marijo Lunt—Did the hitchhiker hold a one-way ticket for Asia?

Eddy Voss—The logger seemed a little too friendly....

George Yerkes—His face was familiar, and kept popping up when least expected.

Chapter One

"Asia, would you like a ride home?" Jeanne Harrison asked as she gathered her things after a long night of inventory. "You look exhausted."

Asia Raferty closed the ledger and faced her assistant manager, an attractive dark-haired woman who at thirty-four was six years older than she.

"Thanks, but no. I've been twisted into a pretzel from so much sitting today." Asia rose from her antique desk, which had been one of her first and favorite finds when she'd started her business. "I need the exercise to work out the kinks."

"That's what you get for being such a slave driver," Jeanne said good-humoredly, stretching and yawning. "You're sure about the ride?"

"Positive."

Since Port Townsend was a small town, Asia wouldn't have far to walk. She never brought her own car to work unless she had a bunch of errands to run.

"See you tomorrow, then," Jeanne called over her shoulder as she sailed out the front door of the shop, the Victorian bell tinkling after her.

Asia fetched her purse from the bottom drawer of her desk, found the antique silver-edged comb she always carried, and pulled it through the tangled strands of her similarly colored silver-blond hair. She dropped the comb back into her bag and straightened her desk top before slipping the bag over her shoulder.

Turning off the lights, she stepped out of the door leading onto Water Street. A quarter moon silvered the town, which had mostly settled down for the night, the antique and bric-a-brac shops having closed hours ago. A few restaurants and bars were still open, their windows gleaming warm and inviting against the cool darkness.

Tired and yet keyed up from working so late, Asia had no desire to go directly home. Usually the pink-trimmed pearl gray Victorian home held an invitation she couldn't resist, but lately she'd been getting restless again.

Since opening Asia's Antiques four years ago, she had taken several trips, and now the urge was getting strong again. Not that she needed more stock for her shop—her general excuse for going on her jaunts—she merely required a temporary change of scene, a little adventure. She was lucky her business was safe in Jeanne's capable hands, she thought, locking the shop door and dropping the keys in her skirt pocket.

For the moment, however, she would settle for a walk longer than the three blocks that would take her to the top of the ridge and home. Tonight the wind's sigh and ocean's swell beckoned as it so often did. A block from the water's edge, she strolled toward the side street that would take her there.

How she loved Port Townsend, perched on the northeastern corner of Washington's Olympic Peninsula, where the waters of the Strait of Juan de Fuca and Puget Sound flowed together. The brightly colored Victorian town was a haven for artists and writers. And tourists who wished they could stay forever.

Crossing deserted Water Street, Asia suddenly had the uneasy feeling that she was being watched.

She slowed and looked over her shoulder to see a man halfway down the block silhouetted by the street lamp behind him. He seemed to be staring after her. Her breath caught in her throat and her step faltered. And then the man slipped into a local bar, the banging door echoing down the street.

Sucking in a lungful of humid, salty air that settled her racing pulse, she went on.

She headed for the end of the cul-de-sac with its small shelter and bench facing the water, a favorite spot where she often ate lunch or dinner, or just came to relax after working late. There she could communicate with nature, replace negative energy with positive.

As she approached the bench, however, the uneasy feeling returned. The sliver of moon was swallowed by clouds, throwing her in absolute darkness. A sudden gust of cold air billowed her long gray skirts around her bare legs and, beneath the cotton eyelet blouse, raised the short hairs on her arms and the flesh along her spine. A silent, intuitive warning raced through her, making her usually steady nerves jangle. Suddenly her friendly refuge turned foreign.

Dangerous.

Was this how her sister Sydney felt when she had one of her premonitions?

As if echoing the water lapping the shore, her senses washed alive and Asia turned to stare back down the cul-de-sac. The short stretch was silent and dark, unlit by a street lamp. She could neither hear nor see anything untoward among the rear entrances and trash collectors she knew to exist on either side of the dead-end street.

Still . . .

Her pulse beat strongly in her throat, pounded thunderously in her ears.

She took a single deep breath of the distinctive salt-water scent, which normally had the power to soothe her, before instinct made her retrace her steps. No reason for her to take unnecessary chances, she told herself, though she had an intrinsic belief that nothing really terrible would ever happen to her.

Fingers clutching the strap of her shoulder bag, she pushed herself toward Water Street. Fast. Not quite running. Her eyes scanning the street ahead. Seeing nothing.

Darkness swirled around her in slow motion.

A metal clatter to her left made her start and cry out. The sound was followed by spitting and threatening yowls. A cat fight. Her lids fluttered in relief, and both her legs and her heart pumped a bit slower when she approached the lighted intersection, now only half a dozen yards ahead.

Her relief was jerked away by fingers like steel closing around her upper arm and whipping her back in the direction from which she'd come.

A strangled scream caught in her throat as she stumbled. "Listen, you can have my purse!" she cried, shoving the thing at the man even as she sensed this was no common mugger.

While one hand held her arm prisoner, the other was a vise on the back of her neck so she couldn't turn her head and see her silent attacker.

"Wait! I can get you some real money!"

But he pushed her inexorably forward, back into the darkness, away from help. Fear flushed through her. Before she could scream, the hand on her neck slipped around to her throat, cutting off her air supply.

A tall, strong woman, she gathered her forces and, holding on to the strap, prepared to use her shoulder bag to fight off her invisible attacker when she had the chance.

She never got it.

They were at the end of the cul-de-sac, mere yards from what she'd thought of as her haven. He jerked her off the sidewalk and forced her behind the building. His knee rammed into the back of hers, popping the joint, throwing her off balance. He kicked her other calf, and the searing pain sent her to the ground without a struggle while her purse tumbled away. Her face pressed into the hard-packed sand with his unbearable weight centered in her back.

She tried to buck him off.

Then he tightened his hold on her throat. Her hands whipped up of their own accord. Savaging his flesh with her nails only increased his pressure on her. Lack of oxygen lighted stars behind her eyes and paralyzed her lungs, which felt ready to burst. Her arms went limp because they could do nothing else. He was strangling her—was going to kill her—and she could do nothing to stop him!

He removed his hand from her throat, his weight from her body. While she choked and coughed as sand ground into her mouth and air painfully filled her lungs, he flipped her over to her back.

"I have a present for you from King Crawley," he whispered hoarsely as she continued to gasp for air.

And then she understood why her brother Dakota had called that morning with some vague warning about letting him know if something out of the ordinary happened to her! He'd said King Crawley was out for revenge because of their father, but he hadn't elaborated! He'd wanted to see her in person to explain what was going on.

Before Asia could muster her reserves, the man was ripping the fragile material of her blouse, exposing her to the night air. Fury accompanied life-giving oxygen and her hands shot out once more, this time toward the face she couldn't see, her nails seeking his eyes.

A deadly sounding click and a sharp, searing pain under her jaw stunned her.

His laugh low and evil, her assailant trailed the point of the switchblade along her throat. "I'd cooperate if I were you," he whispered. "If you want to live, that is."

Fearfully Asia dropped her arms to her sides. This couldn't be happening to her—but it was! Knife still pricking her vulnerable throat, he used his free hand to pull up her skirt to her waist and rip the lace beneath. He was going to rape her! If she fought, he would kill her. Which would be worse? To die fighting or to submit and maybe die anyway?

If she didn't *do* something, she would be another statistic.

She refused to cry, refused to give in without a fight, no matter what the "authorities" suggested. He wasn't the typical assailant who might be scared off by threat of disease or pretended insanity. What could she do against a larger man's strength? Against a knife? Oh, Lord, she couldn't believe she was a helpless victim...a woman who prided herself on her quick-wittedness and strength!

The metallic sound of his zipper screamed through her body, ripped her very core. She wouldn't let it happen! She clawed the hard-packed sand on either side of her, dug deep, grasped all she could, flung the sand at the outline of his head while jerking up both knees in an attempt to unseat him.

"Don't fight it!" he yelled, his knife hand slackening.

She grabbed the opportunity—and his wrist—and screamed for all she was worth! A fist crashed against the side of her head, bringing her struggle to an abrupt halt as flashing lights made her mind spin.

He wrenched his knife hand free.

"What's that?" came a query in the distance.

"Got me."

Men's voices. Heavy footsteps. Asia wanted to scream again, but she couldn't focus her energy.

"Hey, is someone hurt?" one of the approaching men called out.

The man above her uttered an oath. His weight lifted from her body, and irrationally, she clawed his shirtfront and tried to stop him from getting away.

"Help!" she croaked as something pinged nearby. "Over here."

With a jerk, her attacker freed himself. He lunged to the side and she barely saw him swoop up her purse before running off into the night, away from the approaching men. Sitting up, she pulled her skirt in place with one hand. With the other she straightened her ripped blouse as the shapes of two men stumbled toward her. The nick under her chin throbbed, and a trickle of blood, warm and sticky, seeped down her neck.

"Are you all right, lady?" a deep voice asked.

The cloud cover parted. Silver light shafted the two young men who stared down at her, one light-haired and tall, one dark and of average height. Neither was too steady on his feet. They'd been drinking. She could smell the liquor. The dark-haired guy extended his hand. Fear shuddered through her, and suspicion scooted her back away from him.

He rocked on his heels and frowned. "I ain't gonna hurt you."

Hugging the ripped material of her blouse to her chest, she scrambled to her feet. "I'm okay. Thanks."

"That your boyfriend?" the other guy asked. "You two have a fight?"

She stared at the blond man as if he were the most stupid creature on earth. She'd almost been raped, and this idiot thought she'd had a falling-out with her boyfriend! She reminded herself that this idiot had saved her from being brutalized, and tempered her response.

"I never saw the man's face. He was a stranger. H-he took my purse."

She was too mortified to explain what her assailant had really tried to do to her, but considering their knowing, concerned expressions, she didn't have to.

"We'll walk you to the police station," the blond guy said kindly.

"Police?"

"You gotta make a report," his friend said.

"Yes, a report," she echoed, her mind racing.

She stumbled toward the sidewalk and he put out a hand to steady her. She tried not to shudder at his touch. As if sensing her fear, he quickly dropped his hand as she regained her balance. And Asia was ashamed, not only of her reaction to his kindness, but of her own stupidity. She should have made Dakota explain his cryptic warning.

And yet nothing her brother had told her on the phone had prepared her for this act of violence. First her sister Sydney had been involved in a scheme meant to drive her to suicide. That aborted plan had been followed by King Crawley's clever attempt to ruin Dakota professionally. So why had she been so brutally attacked?

And what would she tell the local police? Was she supposed to suggest a Seattle racketeer had hired someone to rape her to get even with her father, Judge Jasper Raferty, who put him away? Even though the guys on the force knew her, they might think she was nuts. And if they did believe her, what would be the repercussions for her father?

She still couldn't believe her father had made a bargain with the devil—even if he had reneged at the last minute. To think that King Crawley might have gone free because of her father's weakness, for the promise of money and political connections.

Her mind was spinning as she and her escorts turned onto Water Street. Before she did anything, she wanted to talk to Dakota. He had to know more than he'd told her. She couldn't go to the police until she could sort things out in her mind. And she was certain she was safe for the moment. Her assailant was probably long gone.

That she knew he would be back made her shudder.

"Listen," she said, suddenly stopping. "I, uh, want to get cleaned up first." Unable to look at the men as she lied, she stared at the sidewalk. "Why don't you go ahead to wherever you're staying."

The blond said, "You're making a mistake if you don't report that creep."

"Yeah, you ain't gonna let him get away with what he tried to do to you, are you?"

She met the dark-haired man's sincere gaze and felt the back of her eyelids sting. He was being so kind, and she didn't even know his name.

"No, of course not. I just want to get cleaned up, that's all. Then I'll do something." She could tell by the looks they exchanged that they didn't believe her. "Really."

Not that she'd necessarily go to the police.

"You change your mind, we'll be at the Palace Hotel until noon tomorrow."

"Thank you," Asia said. "Both of you."

And then, still holding on to her ripped blouse, she ran across the street to her shop. Luckily she'd slipped her key ring into her skirt pocket. The two men stood watching her until she was safely inside. She waved to them through the glass and headed for the bathroom.

Trying not to think about what had happened.

But staring at her image in the bathroom mirror, she could do nothing but. She was battered and bruised and bloody.

The shock was so great it took her a moment to notice the sparkle of gold in her hand, and she finally realized she'd been clutching more than her blouse. Letting go of the material, she stared at her open palm, across which lay the object she'd pulled from her attacker's neck.

A gold chain.

She studied it as if it could give her information, but there was nothing special about the plain gold links. Dropping the chain on the sink ledge, she attended to herself.

The knife cut had clotted, but dried blood smeared her throat. A bruise was spreading along her cheekbone where the attacker had punched her, but the worst of it could be covered by her hair, the rest by carefully applied makeup. Then her gaze dropped back to her neck where faint smudges marred the smooth flesh.

She shuddered at the memory it conjured, and she held back hot tears.

She wouldn't cry. No reason. He hadn't succeeded.

Even so, she stripped off every piece of clothing she wore, including the shredded lace bikinis, which she balled and threw away in the wastebasket. And then she cleaned herself with soap and paper towels, scrubbed away the blood and sand and invisible filth the man's hands had left on her body.

She couldn't scrub away the myriad bruises that would be constant reminders of the attack, but she could cover them.

After stepping back into her skirt, Asia pulled on a heavy sweatshirt she always kept around for extra warmth. The blouse joined the lace scraps in the wastebasket. She scraped her fingers through her hair as best she could and blotted the cut that had started bleeding again.

She tried to tell herself she didn't look so bad, but the image reflecting back at her looked like hell.

Now she was about to find out why.

DAKOTA RAFERTY had barely stepped into his loft when the telephone rang.

Noting it was just after midnight, and assuming Honor was calling to say good-night even though he'd just left her place, he picked up the receiver and asked, "Miss me already?"

"This isn't one of your women."

"Asia?" A chill of apprehension shot down Dakota's spine. Usually bubbly and open, his little sister sounded wound up tight as a spring. "What happened?"

"You told me to let you know if anything unusual happened. Well, it did tonight."

He sank down on the arm of a couch. "Asia, are you all right?"

"You knew what he planned to do to me, didn't you?"

A lump formed in the back of his throat. "I was afraid you were going to be attacked—"

"You mean raped, don't you? But why?"

Dakota felt sick inside. He'd tried to protect her, but not hard enough. He threaded his fingers through his dark blond hair and blamed himself for not going after her and dragging her back to Seattle.

"Where are you?"

"At the shop. I'm . . . fine. A little bruised, but a couple of guys came along before . . ."

Dakota got the message and thanked the Lord that Crawley's thug hadn't succeeded.

"I'm sorry I didn't tell you everything, Asia, but that's why I wanted you to come to Seattle."

As usual he'd raised his sister's stubborn streak, and she'd refused. He would have gone to her if he hadn't been so busy with the police and with Honor and her daughter, Nora, who'd been kidnapped as part of Crawley's cruel scheme to get him. He hadn't thought the racketeer would go after Asia so quickly.

"Promise me you'll come home first thing in the morning," he insisted. "I'll meet you at the ferry. Or do you want me to come get you?"

Asia ignored his demand. "How did you know what would happen to me, Dakota?" she asked again. "This time, tell me everything."

Dakota took a deep breath. He'd already explained how King Crawley blamed their father for his family being destroyed. Judge Jasper Raferty had made a deal to disallow evidence at the racketeer's trial, though he hadn't been able to carry through. His conscience had reared, and he'd backed out at the last minute.

Dakota had also warned Asia that Crawley was trying to get revenge through them, the judge's children, but he hadn't revealed the parallels because he hadn't wanted her to panic. A lot of good his caution had done her. Now he had no choice but to explain.

"Crawley decided the best revenge would be to destroy us in the same manner that members of his family were destroyed. His wife, Olive, tried to commit suicide. She failed, but she's not the same woman she once was. So he had Sydney gaslighted, tried to force her to commit suicide. And since his son Dominic was ruined professionally, he tried to ruin me in the same manner. His daughter Jessica—"

"Was raped," Asia said with certainty.

"And she disappeared. No one has seen or heard from her in two years. Crawley's afraid she's dead."

An edge of panic tinged her whispered "Oh, my God."

"You see why I wanted you to come home."

"Port Townsend is my home, Dakota," Asia said in a shaky voice. "And Crawley would have gotten to me no matter where I was. Good Lord, what next? What are we going to do?"

"Get you police protection."

Asia laughed, but the sound was filled with bitterness rather than humor. "For how long? A few days? Weeks? Years? And what if he decides to go after you or Sydney again?"

"Syd has Benno DeMartino to protect her for the moment." Though Dakota didn't expect that relationship to last. Their sister was probably just grateful to the man who had helped her through her ordeal. "I can protect myself."

Usually Asia would have had a quick comeback over a remark like that, implying she couldn't take care of herself. But she was silent, making Dakota realize how truly vulnerable she was.

"Do you think it was the son?" she suddenly asked.

"What?"

"The man who attacked me. What's his name, Dominic?"

"No. Crawley's son is legitimate. He even changed his last name to Crawford so he could get away from the stigma of being a Crawley. The fact that the skeleton was let out of the closet during the trial was what ruined him. People dealing with big money don't want a mobster's son handling it for them."

"The experience could have soured him."

"I had a private investigator check him out."

"So fast?"

"The situation warranted immediate action," Dakota said. "Dominic Crawford is working on the ferry line between Edmonds and Kingston. He was too busy working to have been involved in my problems. I doubt he's responsible for yours.''

''If he's legitimate, maybe he can help.''

''What do you mean, help?''

''He can intercede in our behalf with his father.''

''From what I understand, Dominic Crawford doesn't want anything to do with his father,'' Dakota told her. ''He hasn't visited Crawley in prison once.''

''Maybe it's time he did.''

Dakota didn't like her tone, which was both speculative and determined. ''Stay away from Crawford, Asia,'' he ordered, knowing she would do as she damn well pleased.

Immediately Asia turned the conversation around, putting her brother on the defensive. ''Have you seen Father since the mess with the kidnapping was cleared up?''

''No.''

''Why not?''

Dakota clenched his jaw so he wouldn't say something he would be sorry for. His father had been his idol, the standard to which he'd strived all his life. Now it seemed his standards hadn't been very high, after all.

''Dakota, he's still our father.''

''Pity.''

''Don't say that. You love him. You're just hurt.''

''Aren't you? Don't you realize what happened...almost happened to you tonight was *his* fault?''

''No, Dakota, I put the blame where it belongs,'' Asia said quietly. ''Father loves us and would protect us with his own life if he could. I truly believe that.

King Crawley is a very sick man, and I'm not only talking about the liver cancer that's killing him. The need for revenge can be a cancer as well. A cancer that will eat him alive and ultimately destroy him.''

''If it doesn't destroy the Raferty family first.''

DAKOTA'S STATEMENT echoed through her head the next morning as Asia left home for the Kingston ferry dock at dawn. She'd had plenty of time to think about it all night—she hadn't been able to sleep. Every sound, every creak of the old house had sent her pulse racing. She couldn't live like this—so she was going to do something.

She was going to find Dominic Crawford and beg him to help put an end to his father's vendetta.

On her way through town, she turned her silvery-blue Taurus on the cul-de-sac and parked. Getting out, she slowly approached the area where she'd struggled with the would-be rapist. She peered around carefully as if he might be lying in wait for her to return. Her heart pounded in her breast, the sound echoing in her ears, competing with the outgoing tide.

No one in sight. Too early.

Gray dawn barely lighted the area, while tendrils of fog lingered around the edges of the water. The tide had rippled and smoothed the sand all night. The hard-packed surface was barely ridged. Certainly no sign of an actual struggle. But as her feet touched the ground where she had lain terrified, she put a hand to her throat and gasped. The memory was so vivid she might never be able to erase the pain and fear.

What was she doing here?

Why didn't she turn and get into her car and never come back?

Because she didn't operate that way. Because she was angry. Because she knew she was missing something.

And to grasp what, she had to relive those terrible moments, second by second. The faceless man strangling her, on top of her, running his hands all over her. She shuddered, and sweat trickled down her spine despite the cool morning. Her gorge rose and she was afraid she was going to be sick.

And still she didn't move. She couldn't. Not until she remembered.

She'd dug handfuls of sand, thrown it in the attacker's face, caught his wrist to stop the knife from slicing her. The small wound under her jaw throbbed with the memory, and she started shaking. Choking back a sob, she continued replaying the assault. She remembered screaming. The two slightly drunk tourists coming to investigate. Her assailant swearing, giving up, trying to leave.

She'd grabbed on to his shirt to stop him until he'd ripped himself free.

And back in her shop, she'd found the gold chain in her hand. She slipped it out of her pocket now and stared at the plain links, not an intricate chain to be worn alone. Something must have been hanging from it.

She closed her eyes and concentrated again. She had the man's shirtfront in her fists. Then what? She'd heard a ping! A ping that meant something had gone flying and landed nearby. The something that had been dangling from this chain.

Her eyes whipped open and began searching the sand. The tide, the damnable high tide had shifted the grains, hiding the object that might be some kind of identification. Cursing, she got down on her knees and began smoothing her hands over the hard-packed wet surface, which had been chilled by the cold water. Nothing. She felt nothing but stones of various sizes beaten smooth by the elements.

Frustration rocked her back on her heels for a moment. Then she stood and widened her area of search to include the nearby sidewalk, a stand of wild grass and a tangle of driftwood near the water's edge, just in case the object had flown or been washed farther than she thought.

No luck.

Disgusted, she took a last look around as a wave curled back less than a yard from where she stood. With the toe of her running shoe, she flipped over a clam shell...and was rewarded by a faint glimmer before the water surged back in, wetting her feet.

Down she went onto the wet sand, looking for the glimmer that had disappeared yet again. As the water rolled out, she followed it, her hands lightly smoothing the top layer of sand. Her fingers closed around what felt like a coin, but what she pulled out was a gold medallion little bigger than a quarter. The side facing her was smooth.

Flipping it around, she stared at the raised symbol on the other side—a snake curled around the shaft of what looked like a switchblade knife.

Chapter Two

Both medallion and chain lay snugged in her trouser pocket as Asia parked near the Kingston Ferry terminal. The first ferry of the morning from Edmonds had just pulled in. Knowing the boat wouldn't remain in port long, she jogged toward the dock. A few dozen cars were already lined up, early commuters to the area north of Seattle wandering around or gathering in small knots to chitchat as they waited to board.

Asia passed them and got as close as she could, while cars from the mainland crawled off the boat to solid land. A short way up the dock, a man with his back to her was unloading what looked like boxes of supplies. Muscles rippled across his shoulders as he bent and stretched and lifted. His tanned arms presented a startling contrast to his thin white T-shirt. Drawn to him, Asia averted her eyes from the worn jeans straining across his hips when she realized she was having trouble admiring a well-built hunk as she normally would.

The man who'd tried to rape her had been well-built and far stronger than she....

"Excuse me," she said, the words catching in her throat suddenly gone dry.

She didn't think he heard her and was about to repeat herself when the man straightened and turned. Beneath wavy chestnut hair falling across a strong, broad brow, mocking green eyes drew her measure, making Asia's skin crawl. Would she have this reaction every time a man looked her over with more than casual interest?

"I'm, uh, looking for Dominic Crawford," she said stiffly, and the cynical eyes turned suspicious.

"What for?" the man demanded, looking arrogantly down his straight nose at her.

Not having expected rudeness, Asia stared, then snapped, "That's my concern!" Her discomfort burned away by her rush of anger, she stepped closer. "You could be a bit more civil, you know."

Suspicion withdrew, leaving the green eyes blank of any emotion whatsoever. "So I've been told," he said in a more modulated, almost friendly tone. "What do you want with Crawford?"

"That's none of your business."

"It is if you want me to get him for you."

"It's personal."

The mockery returned. "Personal? You must be one of his women, then."

Asia thought quickly. Agreeing would get her to see Crawford. "Right. So where is he?"

To her irritation, the man ignored her and began hauling supply boxes. She was about to leave and find someone who would help her when, without stopping work, he said, "I'm Crawford—what do you really want?"

Asia swallowed hard as she took in the unyielding expression beneath thick straight eyebrows. "I—I have to talk to you in private."

"No can do, lady. Can't you see I'm busy making a living here?"

She stared at the sensual mouth whose lips seemed carved out of granite. "But this is important," she insisted. "A matter of life and death."

His answer was a look that was both scathing and disbelieving. Asia knew she had to shock him into listening to her. Her heart beat in her throat as she glanced around to make sure no one else was close enough to hear.

"My name is Asia Raferty. My father is the judge who put King Crawley away." She swallowed hard and blurted out the rest. "Your father had one of his goons try to rape me last night. I'm afraid next time I won't get away so lucky."

DOMINIC CRAWFORD FROZE, a crate of at least sixty pounds knotting the muscles in his arms until they screamed with the weight. He set down the box of supplies and stepped around it so he could get a closer look at the blonde with the dark brows arched in plea. She had a sexy mole at the left corner of her luscious full mouth, which for the moment was pinched tight as if its owner were preventing the delectable lips from quivering.

She was covered from ankles to neck in loose gray trousers and a feminine, old-fashioned lace blouse that concealed her neck to her chin and her arms to her wrists. Her silky shoulder-length hair was parted to the side and slid over her right cheek. On closer inspection, he discovered that the delicate alabaster skin under the silver strands was skillfully covered with makeup. Even so, the telltale flush of a bruise shone through. He realized the blouse, too warm for the unusually hot summer day, undoubtedly hid others. And a flesh-colored bandage taped the soft flesh under her jaw.

What really got him, however, were the slightly tilted eyes—a soft gray blue—openly vulnerable and filled with an underlying dread he recognized all too well.

"All right," he finally said, brutally shoving thoughts of his sister to the back of his mind for the thousandth time. "I can't talk here. How about meeting me after work—"

"But that could be too late!" she interrupted, dread turning into something akin to panic.

Dominic cursed softly. He couldn't afford to lose this job. And yet he couldn't just leave the woman to cool her heels when she was so obviously upset, not when his father was involved. What the hell was the old man up to now from behind his prison bars?

"Wait here."

He left her staring after him. He could sense that pale gaze boring into his back as if she were trying to assess him. He was used to the feeling. People had been sitting in judgment of him all his life. He'd escaped such close scrutiny for years at a time, but whenever he finally thought he was safe, life played one of its nasty little tricks on him.

He found his boss and ticked the man off with his request for an extended break. One round-trip of the ferry—an hour and twenty minutes—was all he asked. Grudgingly, old Hank came through but told him he'd lose pay for the time and that he'd better be waiting for the ferry before it even docked again if he wanted to keep his job.

Dominic agreed and sprinted back to where Asia Raferty waited, her expression anxious.

"Give me a minute," he told her.

He grabbed one of the last two crates from the ferry and set it on the dock. He knew she was watching his every move as he finished up and the captain loudly signaled his intention to leave. He stepped back as the separation between boat and dock grew wider.

"Let's go get a cup of coffee," he said, taking Asia's arm to guide her.

Her reaction was totally unexpected and shook him to the core. She cried out and backed away. Her face paled, her tilted eyes rounded, her willowy body shuddered. She was having trouble breathing, keeping control. Then she seemed to come to her senses.

"I—I'm sorry."

The words came out a choked whisper, and embarrassment stained her too-white face.

"Come on."

This time he kept a foot or more distance between them as he led the way to Waterview Café, deserted now that the commuter ferry was chugging across Puget Sound. They took a booth in the back and, while the owner remained behind the counter watching some early-morning talk show, they sipped coffee from mugs.

Rather, Dominic drank while Asia stared into the dark liquid swirling with the nervous movement of her hand.

"I only have an hour," he told her when he'd half drained the mug and she still hadn't gone into her pitch. "So tell me what happened and why you think my..." About to say "father," he changed it to "Why you think King Crawley was behind this attack on you?''

She turned anxious eyes on him. "I don't think. I know. He's already plied his sick vengeance on my sister and brother. Last night, my turn began. I'm not naive enough to think it's over just because the attempt was a failure.''

Dominic tried his best to remain removed, but as Asia Raferty told him her story, starting with the aborted deal between their two fathers and ending with her close escape of the night before, he sickened as he always did when confronted by his parent's misdeeds.

As a child he'd loved and been close to his father, but age had brought a crack in the relationship that Dominic's maturing morality had widened. He hadn't been able to understand or condone the illicit and immoral things King Crawley had been involved in, and so he had put a physical distance between him and his father.

Eventually the distance had grown into an uncrossable chasm—his disavowal of King Crawley's very existence. As far as he knew, the feeling was mutual, and Dominic wanted to keep the status quo. He'd been doing all right for the past couple of years after losing everything he'd worked so hard for. But now Asia Raferty was once more making him face up to something he didn't want to see and couldn't understand— that a man who could be supposedly loving with the members of his own family could be unspeakably brutal with anyone who crossed him.

''I'm sorry,'' Dominic said, staring into eyes that shone with unshed tears.

Asia was holding a brave front but he wondered how little it would take to shatter her completely. He wanted to cover her trembling hand with his but was afraid of her reaction. He couldn't stand to see her shake with fear as she had when he'd simply tried to take her arm earlier.

"I wish I could do something."

"You can," she said eagerly. "That's why I had to find you. I was hoping you would help me."

"How?"

"Talk to your father—"

"I don't have a father. I haven't had one in years."

Her heartfelt curse startled him and he stared.

"You sound like my brother, Dakota," she explained. "He won't acknowledge our father, either."

"I don't blame him."

"Well, I do!"

Dominic wearily passed his hand over his eyes. "You can't change someone because you don't like what they are."

"But you can try."

He'd tried. God, how he'd tried. But his father had said he was still wet behind the ears, with no concept of the real world and what it took to survive. Dominic had been fifteen, maybe sixteen, at the time. And the chasm had begun.

"I can't," he said with a resigned sigh. "I really am sorry."

He rose and put a hand to his pocket to pay for the coffee. Quicker than he, Asia stayed his hand with her own. Her nails dug into him like the claws of a desperate animal.

"*Please....*"

With her face raised, her hair fell back, revealing the ugly reality of what his father's man had done to her. The side of her face was not only badly bruised, but the flesh was swollen. Reluctantly he sank back into his side of the booth. He pitied her. She didn't understand that he couldn't do anything to help her.

"I can't help you," he said aloud.

She'd relaxed a little, but her hand was still touching his as if with her very will she could prevent him from trying to leave. After the display on the dock, he had some idea of how much it took for her to touch him at all.

"You can talk to him," she said softly. "Ask him to stop this vendetta of his."

"He wouldn't listen."

"You're his son."

"I *was* his son." Dominic shook his head. "I made the separation so long ago, being his son is like a dream. And a nightmare. I haven't lived in his house or taken his money since I was eighteen. I changed my name at twenty-one. I didn't want to be a Crawley, and he gave me his good riddance. I barely saw him after that—only when I went to visit my mother and sister. I haven't seen him at all since the trial."

Her expression was that of a desperate woman as she finally let go of him and shrank back into the booth. "So what am I supposed to do?" Her voice was soft, barely more than a whisper. "Sit around and wait for one of his men to succeed in raping me the way your sister was?"

The reference to Jessica was like a slap in the face. One he deserved, Dominic knew, but that didn't stop his anger.

"You don't know anything about Jess." His staccato words were low and controlled, unlike the wild beating of his heart when he thought about what had happened to his little sister, the person in the world he most loved and who had loved him without condition. "She was the sweetest, most gentle young woman on the face of this earth. What happened to her was an atrocity. Being brutalized by that animal who was our father's enemy tore her apart, killed her... at least figuratively."

"And what?" She raised her chin. "You think I could just toss off the same thing happening to me?"

"That's not what I meant."

"It's a little difficult to understand anything about you, Dominic Crawley Crawford—whoever you may be." Asia's voice rose as did the emotion that painted her features with a life he hadn't heretofore seen. "You profess to hate your father's actions, and yet you're willing to sit by and let him continue until he—"

"I told you I couldn't stop him."

"—until he destroys every member of my family, starting with me," she went on, right over his words. "Will you feel better, then? Quid pro quo? Is that it? One member of my family destroyed for each of yours? Will what happened to your sister seem less horrible if she has company? Are you really more like your father than you want to admit?"

Dominic was tempted to slap her then. How dare she intimate he had anything in common with King Crawley! He was nothing like the man who had spawned him.

Nothing!

That she would dare to make the comparison lighted a deep-burning fuse that wouldn't easily be extinguished. The insult would be one he wouldn't likely forgive or forget. He'd spent his entire adult life driving that blasted wedge, separating himself not only from his father but virtually from the rest of his family, as well.

"You don't understand a damn thing!" he accused.

"I think I do." She leaned into the table and toward him. "You won't help me any more than you helped your own sister after she was attacked, isn't that right?"

He lost it then, and with a sweep of a powerful hand sent his mug flying off the table to crash into the opposite wall. The container splintered into a hundred shards, staining the already grimy wall with dripping brown liquid.

"Hey, what in tarnation's going on?" the owner asked, drawn by the noise for a moment from his television set.

"An accident," Dominic stated.

Unable to trust in his own ability to keep control of his temper, he slid out of the booth and turned his back on Asia Raferty. Digging in his pocket, he pulled out a twenty-dollar bill and placed it on the counter.

"This should cover your trouble," he told the owner.

Then he stalked out the door without looking back.

Halfway to the dock, however, he realized he wasn't alone. Asia was after him like a bulldog after a bone. Her long legs easily caught up with his.

"You want to get yourself hurt, lady?" he growled without bothering to glance her way.

"I already have been hurt." She grabbed him by the arm, and to his surprise spun him to a stop with the incredible strength of one possessed. "That was a low blow, saying what I did. I apologize. Maybe you couldn't do anything for your sister, Jessica, but can't you please think of something to help me and my family?"

"I don't owe you anything."

"No, you don't."

Her expression was honest, her eyes searching. He could imagine them inside him, peering around, judging.

"But maybe you owe yourself," she continued. "Maybe instead of hiding behind a fake name and running away from who you are, you can stand up and be counted. Fight back for once in your life instead of trying to hide from what you can't change."

She shamed him, then. As terrified as the woman was, she wasn't quitting or slinking off to lick her wounds. She was doing what she could to save herself, to save her family, by meeting the problem as head-on as she knew how.

Still, what *could* he do, even if he agreed to help? Dominic asked himself.

"Jess." Her name passed his lips again, and it echoed the grief he'd been nursing since she'd disappeared two years before. "My sister might be able to change the old man's mind. He had a soft spot for her, used to say she was the sunshine of his heart."

"Do you know where she is?"

"Maybe dead."

"Do you believe that?"

Dominic shook his head. No, he'd never believed Jess was dead, not deep inside himself. He'd gone after her when she'd disappeared, but he'd given up her trail too easily. And the guilt of his own impotence had been eating at him ever since.

"I figured she wanted to disappear, to start over. The animal who raped her wouldn't let her alone. He was giving King Crawley the high sign by threatening his daughter, something he wouldn't dare to have done while the old man was free. I figured Jess wanted a new life, removed from the danger—and stigma—of being King Crawley's daughter. I understood only too well. I let her."

"And now you regret it."

Her touch on his arm gentled, as did her expression, and Dominic could tell she felt sorry for him. His gut twisted something queer. With all her troubles, Asia Raferty felt sorry for him.

"Yeah, I regret a lot of things."

"It's not too late to make a difference, Dominic. We can find her—"

"How?"

"We can find her, and you can love and protect her. And maybe she can stop the cancer eating at your father's heart."

"You expect too much from me," he stated honestly. "Don't. I'll only let you down."

"We can do it together. I know we can. We have to." She was speaking calmly, as if she were trying to convince herself as much as him. "It's up to us to stop your father, Dominic. I can try, but I don't know if I can do it alone. Will you help me? Please?"

He struggled with his conscience. He could turn his back on her.

He'd had lots of practice.

All these years he'd thought himself courageous— going out into the world alone at eighteen, making his own way, building a new life—but she'd kicked that notion right out from under him as easily as a shaky stool. For once he was honest with himself. He'd taken the coward's way out, first by turning his back on both his parents rather than fighting his father, then by letting his sister down when she needed him most.

What the hell kind of a man was he?

If only he could have Jess back in his life, maybe he could be different. Better.

He gave Asia a long, assessing look. Real courage warred with the fear in her eyes. She wasn't going to give up until she got herself killed. He could sense that foolish tenacity in her. Then her death would be one more mark on his conscience, one more guilt to plague him for the rest of his miserable, lonely life.

How the hell was he going to live with himself if he let that happen?

"I'll help you," he said, his agreement signing the death warrant of "Dominic Crawford."

While he might keep the phony name, which was, in fact, legally his, he knew that to win the game he had to be honest, at least with himself.

He would have to become what he most dreaded: his father's son.

KING CRAWLEY PACED the small, dank visitation room—and carefully plotted his next move. Slumped at the door, the guard sat there quietly. He was well paid to close his eyes and ears when Crawley wanted privacy.

Where was Lester Freidman?

The need for revenge filled his every waking moment, haunted his every dream. It was the energy that fueled him, that made him refuse the paltry treatments the doctors deemed necessary. He would have Judge Raferty on his knees the next time he met his adversary, and that would be satisfaction enough to send Crawley to the next world with a smile on his lips.

He briefly wondered if anyone would mourn him.

His wife was lost in her own world, possibly too lost to understand when he finally gave in to the liver cancer that was killing him. His daughter was gone, probably dead herself. Maybe he'd be able to see her, if only for a moment in the hereafter, before his soul was consigned to hell. Dominic was the only one left to mourn him, but Crawley was afraid his only son—the son he loved more than life itself, just as he had his sweet daughter—would be glad instead.

The thought hurt like hell. How had the rift grown so wide between them? Why hadn't he stopped it? Why hadn't he at least tried?

Pride.

He'd let his damnable pride get in the way of making his son see reason, or allowing himself to compromise. Dominic had rejected him, and Crawley hadn't been able to swallow the fact that his own son had held ethics and morality in higher esteem than the love of his own parent.

Not that he'd stopped loving Dominic, no matter what his son believed in.

The bond between them was forever. Crawley had let Dominic go his own way, but he'd always been there, looking over his shoulder—not in person, but via one of his men. Through the years, he'd seen to his son's safety, had known every move he'd made, had celebrated his many successes and commiserated with his few failures. He'd been proud of all that Dominic had built, that he had the courage and tenacity to be his own man.

And he was sick every time he thought about all that Dominic had lost because of him.

Because of Jasper Raferty, he amended.

Burying that depressing thought, he checked the wall clock to see how late Freidman was, even as the door opened. More than ten minutes.

"Where the hell have you been?" he demanded of the erstwhile accountant, who was in reality his right-hand man. "You know how I despise waiting."

Freidman didn't flinch. "Traffic. Someone ought to keep those southern Californians from moving to Seattle. They're taking over the town."

"Not my part of the town," Crawley growled. "And that's what's important."

Freidman shrugged his thin shoulders and threw himself into a chair at the table. Crawley didn't like his attitude, which had changed for the worse since he'd spent a piddling night in jail because of Dakota Raferty. Freidman was out on bail until the trial, and Crawley was certain the charges against him wouldn't stick.

The accountant hadn't been directly involved in kidnapping the Bright dame's daughter, or in getting his hands on the salmon-fishing files, the use of which would have ruined Dakota Raferty's career for good. Janet Ingel wouldn't implicate Freidman if she knew what was good for her. The ambitious lobbyist might have lost her step up in the world, but she still had her life to look forward to, even if a few years of it would be spent behind bars. And his man Vinny had successfully eluded the authorities to continue the cause.

"You spoke to Vinny?" he asked impatiently.

Crawley didn't like the way Freidman avoided his eyes as he nodded in confirmation. His gut twisted as he pounced on the colorless man.

"And?"

Glancing at the guard, Freidman kept his voice low. "She managed to get away. He almost had her but a couple of tourists bungled by and ruined everything."

Ruined everything.

The words echoed through Crawley's head until he thought he would lose his mind. How could his plans be foiled again? He felt as if he were ready to explode.

"We'll have to alter the original plan yet again," Freidman was saying.

"Screw the plan!" Crawley hissed, furious that Asia Raferty had slipped neatly through his hands, as had her siblings.

He quickly made up his mind. He'd been thwarted long enough. He wouldn't see yet another Raferty go unpunished. He would get them all in one swift stroke that would leave them reeling. They would never forget the length of his reach, the purity of his purpose.

Especially not the judge who'd double-crossed him. Jasper Raferty would shrivel up and die inside as Crawley had done when each member of his family had been destroyed by his trial and subsequent incarceration.

"Asia Raferty is a dead woman," Crawley stated stonily, unmoved by the brief flicker of dread that crossed Freidman's face. "Arrange it. Have her killed . . . and anyone else who gets in the way!"

Chapter Three

Somewhat shocked that she'd gotten Dominic's support after the way he'd blown up at her, Asia waited for him in the car when the ferry pulled in and he went to tell his boss that he was taking the rest of the day off. Hopeful that together they could indeed find a way to neutralize his father's vindictiveness, she only wished she could trust Dominic fully.

Her stomach took a queer little turn as she spotted him stalking toward her. He was a fine-looking man, would be quite handsome if his face weren't wreathed in a threatening scowl. A thread of fear needled through her and just as quickly dissipated. She wasn't the cause of his ire this time.

Besides, as angry as she'd made him earlier, he hadn't tried to hurt her.

Not every man wanted to hurt her, she told herself, hand slipping to her throat. Dull pain at her own light touch made her remember the one who had. She jerked her hand away and the memory aside. She wanted to believe in human decency as desperately as she wanted to regain her lost innocence, her intrinsic belief that nothing too terrible to bear would ever touch her.

Without a word, Dominic threw himself in the passenger seat and slammed the door. He was so angry he was practically smoking.

"I guess your boss wasn't too happy with your taking the day off?"

"I guess not, considering he fired me."

"Fired . . ." Asia closed her eyes and touched her forehead to the steering wheel. "This is my fault. Dominic, I'm—"

"Don't worry about it."

But she could tell *he* did. She heard the truth of the matter in his voice. He didn't want any apologies, so she wouldn't offer him another. But she was sorry. He'd lost a whole life because of who his father was, and now because of her, he didn't even have a simple means of supporting himself, while back in Port Townsend, Jeanne was once again holding down the fort for her.

"So where do we start?" she asked.

"By getting on this ferry. We're going to pay my mother a visit. If Jess contacted anyone about her whereabouts, it would be Mother."

If Jessica was still alive, an inner voice taunted.

Of course Dominic's sister was alive, Asia assured herself—Jessica *had* to be alive and able to soften Crawley, not only for herself but for the rest of her family.

Her positive thoughts kept her calm as the ferry plied Puget Sound. They got out and walked around the deck, Asia happy to expend some of her nervous energy. Silent and brooding, Dominic didn't say more than a few words to her until they were in Edmonds, and then only to give her directions to the Crawley residence in Seattle's Magnolia area.

The lovely waterfront Tudor home stood on a high bluff. The view of Puget Sound and the Olympic Mountains was not unlike that from the Raferty home on neighboring Queen Anne's Hill, where Asia grew up and her father still lived.

The difference in atmosphere was notable, however. Where her family's brick colonial was graced by nothing more imposing than English gardens, the Crawley estate was surrounded by a high brick security wall. Barbed wire curled along the top, and they entered the grounds through a wrought iron gate opened electronically from inside the house only after Dominic identified himself.

Asia pulled onto the wide, curved drive and parked opposite the house. No sooner had they stepped out of the car than the front door opened. Dressed in a lightweight gray suit, a tall, thin man with a shock of white hair stood waiting for them.

"Mr. Dominic, how good to see you."

The elderly man's brown eyes turned to Asia in question. If she thought Dominic might introduce her, she was wrong.

"Ian, we're here to see my mother," was all Dominic said. "How is she today?"

"The same, I'm afraid," Ian said, his voice lowered. He stood back to let them enter, stating, "I shall tell Mrs. Crawley you're here."

"You don't have to tell me anything, Ian," a woman stated blithely.

Dominic turned toward the nearby staircase. "Hello, Mother."

Appearing to be in her early to mid-fifties, Olive Crawley was a woman of average height, slight build and delicate features, giving her something of a fragile air. She swept down the stairs, a gauzy pastel floral-print dress floating around her. Asia quickly took in the thick chestnut hair lightly silvered at the temples and green eyes so like her son's.

"Dom, you're home." Olive put out her arms and lifted her cheek for his embrace and kiss. "Such a pleasant surprise. You should have called." She pulled away and frowned at his T-shirt and jeans. "And dressed more appropriately. You young people." Then she turned to inspect Asia carefully. "And what a pretty companion. Are you a college schoolmate of Dominic's, dear?"

Asia blinked in confusion. "School—"

"This is Asia, Mother," Dominic smoothly interrupted. "She's a new friend."

His mother's smile was sunny and sweet. "Well, we must get better acquainted, then, perhaps over tea. You do drink tea, don't you, Asia?"

"Yes, of course."

"Ian, would you see to it," Olive Crawley graciously demanded. "We'll be on the garden terrace."

"Very good, Mrs. Crawley."

The butler strode off toward an open doorway that led into the dining room and, no doubt, the kitchen beyond.

Asia remembered Dakota telling her Olive Crawley had been driven to the edge by her husband's trial and incarceration, had tried to commit suicide and had never regained her full faculties. That she imagined her son was still in school confirmed that bit of information, making Asia suspect visiting her would be a waste of time.

Resigned to making the best of the circumstances, she followed Olive straight through the house, with

Dominic directly behind her. The terrace overflowed with potted flowering plants of brilliant hue that surrounded white wrought-iron furniture. The view was magnificent, but Asia's perception of it was marred by the distinct feeling of being watched. No doubt hidden security cameras covered every portion of the house and grounds.

No sooner had Asia touched down in the cushioned chair than Olive asked, "Where did you and my son meet if not in school? He keeps telling me he's too busy for a social life."

Not knowing what else to say, Asia told the truth. "Uh, we met at the ferry dock."

"How romantic."

Asia gave Dominic a quick look when he didn't deny that. His expression was enigmatic.

"Mother, you've done a wonderful job with your plants this year."

He kept her distracted and talking about trivial things until Ian carried out a silver service and delicate porcelain cups and plates. Obviously at home playing the gracious lady of the manor, Olive poured tea and served scones with clotted cream and strawberry jam. Asia made a pretense of enjoying the treat, while keeping tight rein on her rising nerves and wondering how long they would be stuck there.

So when Dominic casually asked, "Mother, have you heard from Jess?" Asia was startled out of her complacency.

A frown twitched across Olive's forehead for a second, marring its delicate beauty. She seemed to turn inward, smiled softly, and her brow smoothed, giving Asia hope that they might get somewhere with the confused woman, after all.

"Jessica always was such a lovely girl," Olive said softly. "I remember when she was born. Such a tiny thing to occupy such a large space in my heart."

"Mine, too, Mother," Dominic reassured her. He patted her fragile-looking hand, then engulfed it in his large, rough-looking one. "But have you seen her lately?"

Olive thought about the question for a moment, sipping her tea. "Jess hasn't been by the house lately."

Asia let out the breath she'd been holding.

"Children sometimes don't do what their parents think is best for them," Olive added.

"What did you think was best for your daughter?" Asia asked, unable to keep the impatience from her tone.

Olive blinked as if startled, as if she'd forgotten she had a guest. "I—would you like more tea?"

"We don't want more tea," Dominic said firmly. "We want to know where Jess is."

Her response—"Why didn't you say so?"—nearly knocked Asia off her chair.

"You know where your daughter is, then?" she asked.

"No."

Asia couldn't help herself. She let out a little moan that drew a black look from Dominic.

"But Peggy might be able to tell you."

"Peggy," Dominic echoed as Asia's hopes were raised yet again. "I don't remember Jess having a friend named Peggy."

"You don't know everything, Dom." Olive turned to Asia. "These sassy young men think they know more than their parents."

"He'll learn better," Asia said, playing along. "Maybe Peggy can teach him. Where can we find her?"

"I don't remember."

"Try, Mother. This is important."

Obviously catching the urgency in his tone, Olive looked distressed. "Oh, dear, something is wrong, isn't it?"

"Everything will be just fine if I can talk to Jess. That's why I'm looking for her. Who is this Peggy?"

"Peggy Shield," she said, as if that would explain everything. "She wrote to me a few times so I would know Jessica was all right."

Hallelujah! Jessica was alive! At least they'd learned that much. Asia connected with Dominic's green gaze and the succeeding jolt hit her hard.

He disconnected and turned back to his mother. "Can you show me one of Peggy's letters?"

"Now, Dom, I've always taught you it's not polite to read other people's mail."

"Only when they don't give me permission," he countered. "Please, I'm asking you to let me see them."

"Well, I guess it wouldn't hurt anything. I keep them in my parlor." Smoothing her skirts as she rose, Olive added, "I shall be but a moment."

"Shouldn't we go with her?" Asia whispered as soon as the other woman was out of earshot.

"Let's wait and see what she finds."

She glanced toward the terrace doors, but movement beyond caught her eye. A dark, furtive shape among the greenery. When she gave the area her complete attention, however, she saw no one and wondered if she'd been imagining things.

"Could someone be watching us?"

"More than likely." Though he didn't seem perturbed, Dominic turned in his seat, then glanced back at her. "There used to be more bodyguards than family members before . . ." He let the rest of the statement drop. "Mother is still being protected."

The idea that their every move might be under personal scrutiny gave Asia the creeps. The idea of security cameras had been bad enough. Since she could do nothing about the situation, she attempted to shake off the feeling.

"Do you think we'll find anything in these letters that'll lead us to your sister?"

"Since it's the only thing we've got, let's hope so."

They were both relieved when Olive left the house to rejoin them, a blue envelope in hand. Her brow was furrowed again, when she said, "I can't seem to remember what I did with the others. This one came just last month."

Dominic took the offering from his mother and slid out a single sheet of stationery paper. Asia watched his eager expression dim. He looked up at her and shook his head.

"Not a clue. She just says Jess is fine and sends her love. No indication of where she might be or what she's doing."

He flipped over the envelope so she could see Olive's name and address neatly typed. No return address.

Dejected, she was about to suggest they leave when she thought of something. "The postmark."

"Of course." Dominic held up the envelope for closer inspection. "It's pretty light." He squinted. "Eagle Creek—that's it!"

"On the Olympic Peninsula!" Asia added. She was so excited she could have hugged Dominic.

Almost.

Unbidden, a scene flashed through her mind—her attacker's weight levered over her thighs, his hands groping—and she wasn't certain she would ever be comfortable in a man's arms again.

WHAT WAS THE DAUGHTER of Judge Jasper Raferty doing in King Crawley's home? With King Crawley's son? Seeing her there with Dominic and his mother had been a shock, and instinct had prompted the watcher to stay alert.

But Asia Raferty had grown uncomfortable and had realized she was under scrutiny. Withdrawing for the moment had seemed most expedient since remaining undetected was of paramount importance. The judge's whelp had relaxed, had no idea she was being watched from the shadows of the mansion as she reentered it with Dominic, while Olive Crawley remained on the terrace with her tea and scones and confused memories.

What was going on?

Though Dominic had strayed from the fold, he'd never betrayed one of his own before.

"I think we should leave for Eagle Creek immediately," Asia said in a low voice as they crossed through the living room.

"Not so fast. No one says finding this Peggy Shield is going to solve everything. Who knows where Jessica might be, how far we'll have to travel to find her?"

"Then the sooner we get started the better."

"We'll take some extra clothes. We can swing by my place first and pick up the Bronco while we're at it," Dominic stated, crossing the foyer and holding open the door. "Four-wheel drive might come in handy out on the peninsula."

Asia Raferty didn't looked pleased at the suggestion, and yet she didn't argue as she preceded Dominic out of the house. The door closed softly behind them, and lurking in the shadows became unnecessary. Going to the window, the watcher gazed after them thoughtfully.

Jessica ... they thought she was alive?

The name Peggy Shield registered as did the town of Eagle Creek. They wouldn't be the only ones making a trip to the peninsula.

DOMINIC GAVE a low whistle as he jumped out of the Bronco, which he'd pulled in back of Asia's smaller car. The pearl gray, pink-trimmed Victorian building reminded him of the woman who owned it. Classy and understated yet clearly eye-appealing.

"Some house."

"I fell in love the first time I saw it." Asia led the way up to the wraparound porch and the door inset with an oval of beveled glass. "Of course the paint was peeling and this porch was falling apart, among other little inconveniences."

As he stepped inside, Dominic felt a sense of welcome ... almost as if he were personally invited to be part of the warm, comfortable life Asia had made for herself. Antique wooden furniture glowed next to plain modern sand-colored couches. Rays of the sun through intricate beveled glass insets in the bay windows shot rainbows over both the furniture and the myriad plants placed strategically around the room.

"You've done a hell of a job fixing it up."

"I always put one hundred percent into anything I do," she told him, heading for the staircase set to one side of the vestibule. "Maybe that's why I've never failed. It'll only take me a few minutes to pack and make a couple of calls. I have to let my assistant manager know I'll be gone for a while." Already climbing the steps, she paused and her brow pulled into a frown. "And whether or not I want to, I have to call Dakota."

"Your brother?"

She nodded, her silky blond hair swaying against her bruised cheek. "He won't like it, but he's got to know what I'm doing."

"You're going to tell him you're with me?"

"Yes."

"That should give him a stroke."

"My brother knows I can take care of myself," she said, annoyance crossing her face. "Dominic, I want you to understand I don't quit because something gets tough. We have to find your sister." She moved up the stairs, saying, "I promise I won't give up until we do."

Watching her disappear on the second floor, Dominic didn't answer. He didn't want to shatter Asia's belief in herself with the kind of negative thinking that came to him all too easily these days. Maybe she would succeed where he had failed. Or maybe contact with her indomitable spirit was what he needed to recover what he'd lost in the past couple of years.

As ridiculous as it sounded, they were a lot alike—he the son of a racketeer, she the daughter of a judge. Asia wouldn't believe that, not after what she knew about his background, after seeing him working at a menial job. But he'd had her brand of confidence once. He'd lost it along with everything else he'd held in value—wife, home, profession.

Overnight he'd gone from success to failure.

Though he'd told himself he hadn't cared, he had— only not enough to fight. After struggling all his adult life with who he was and who he wanted to be, he'd been bone weary of the conflict. So he'd lost himself in the business of surviving, had convinced himself he was content.

And so, for the past two years, he'd lived a lie.

His heart's desire was to make a new life, find someone special with whom to share it, do something for a living that gave him satisfaction—and in a place where no one cared about his name. He wanted to be accepted for himself, for who *he* was, as impossible as he knew that to be.

Simply put, he wanted to be happy again. Or, perhaps, really happy for the first time since he'd found out what his father did for a living.

First, he had to neutralize his father's powerful reach.

"Oh, Jess, I have to find you for both our sakes. Maybe we can help each other."

He was staring out the front window at the surrounding brilliantly painted Victorian houses—none of which held a candle to Asia's in simplicity and appeal—when he heard her light footsteps on the stairs.

He turned to find her carrying a soft-sided bag in one hand, a medium-weight jacket in the other. And though she still wore the same gray trousers, she'd sensibly changed out of the fancy lace blouse into an oversize soft coral pocket T-shirt. A scarf in contrasting Southwestern colors wrapped her throat, undoubtedly camouflaging bruises.

"I'm ready if you are."

Something deep inside Dominic stirred when she smiled warmly at him, despite the fear and pain and distrust she must be experiencing. It was then he vowed he would see the venture through—fight his father at last, if in a different arena than he might have chosen—not only for Jess and himself, but for one brave if misguided woman named Asia Raferty.

JUDGE JASPER RAFERTY felt his heart beat furiously against his rib cage as Dakota related the aborted rape attempt on his younger daughter, the latest in a series of events triggered by King Crawley's insane need for vengeance. He should have known when the first two attempts to destroy him through Sydney and Dakota had failed that Crawley would shift his attentions to Asia.

"And now she's gone off with Crawley's son to find a woman who is believed to be dead," Dakota was saying. "She wouldn't listen to reason."

"My God, poor Asia," Sydney murmured, her pale gray eyes stricken. "I knew I should have called—"

"Knew?" Dakota interrupted.

She shifted a quick, uneasy look at her father. "I, uh, had one of those dreams—"

"Nonsense!" Jasper shouted. He forced himself to keep his hands on the arms of his chair and away from his chest, which was beginning to tighten unnaturally. He took a deep calming breath, but he was beginning to feel hot all over, and his left arm felt strange.

"Please, Sydney," he said in a calmer tone, "don't start with the psychic thing. This is serious business."

"She knows this is serious," Dakota returned stiffly, barely glancing at him.

Jasper wished he could reach out and touch his son, but since Dakota had found out about the deal he'd made with Crawley—one he hadn't even carried through—his son had shunned him as a pariah. Jasper knew the only reason Dakota deigned to step foot in the Raferty home was due to his worry for his sister. In times of crisis, the Rafertys didn't hesitate to rally for one another, even if that meant putting personal differences aside for the moment.

Jasper wondered if Dakota would come to him if he were the one who needed help. The unobvious answer troubled him.

"What are we going to do, Dakota?" Sydney whispered, her large eyes and round cheeks appearing almost childlike surrounded by wisps of short hair.

"Pray, Syd, and hope to God that Asia is all right."

With that, Dakota gave his own father a look that pierced Jasper's already ailing heart.

The judge awkwardly pushed himself up from his chair, muttering, "While you two are praying, I'm going to do something more tangible."

"Father, where are you going?" Sydney asked, though he could see by her eyes she'd already guessed.

"I'm going to face Crawley and see if I can't find a way to make him take out his spite on the person who earned it instead of on the innocent."

"Father!" Sydney cried, sounding utterly appalled. "Please, don't go."

Holding his left side stiffly, Jasper moved to the front door, waiting for Dakota to call him back.

The words never came.

With a lump in his throat, he left the house for the steady drizzle of a Seattle day. Somehow he stumbled to his car and got behind the wheel. Then he had to wait until his arm relaxed, his chest stopped squeezing and he could breathe normally again.

After a few minutes, he started the car and went forth to meet his enemy.

While driving to the prison, he recounted his professional life. All the good he had done as a judge. The vicious criminals he'd kept off the streets. The innocent people he'd protected.

He'd slipped from his bench once.

He hadn't been able to go through with the deal that would have revitalized his failed fortune and safeguarded the family home for future generations, the deal that would have advanced his political career and brought him honor for all that he had done in society's behalf. In the end, he realized the means weren't justifiable, and he hadn't been able to turn scum like Crawley back loose on an unsuspecting public.

About to face Crawley for the second time in as many weeks—and only the second time since he'd sentenced him more than two years before—Jasper was as nervous as he was angry. Their last session had left him feeling like a fool. The experience was still fresh in his gut.

"Judge Raferty, what a surprise!" Crawley said as he entered the narrow visiting room where Jasper waited standing at a table. He stuck out his barrel chest. "And to what do I owe this honor?"

Waving the guard out of the room, he said, "Cut the innocent routine, Crawley. You know why I'm here!"

"Do I?"

"I asked you once before . . . now I'm telling you—lay off my family!"

"Or you'll what?" Crawley asked innocently. "Gonna slap my hands? Give me a coupla more years. Be my guest. I won't live long enough to enjoy them. The doctors say if I don't start treatment, I might not be around to see the tulips push up the dirt in the spring."

Once again Jasper realized he had no hold over Crawley. There was nothing he could threaten the man with to make him stop taking out his vengeance on the innocent. There was nothing he could do . . . unless he could get the racketeer to enter into a bargain. He would trade his very life if he were guaranteed his children would be safe.

"What do you want?" Jasper asked, renewed stirrings in his chest making him shift with discomfort.

He was going to have to see the doctor first thing in the morning. He hadn't been feeling well for the past week, not since he'd realized his children were being punished for his own weakness and Dakota had disowned him as a parent.

Crawley leaned over the table, fists pressed against the surface. His rawboned face pulled into a downright mean expression that left no room for compromise.

"I wanna see you lose everything important to you . . . just like I did."

"I've already lost my son. Isn't that enough?"

Crawley laughed, and the desire to strangle the loathsome vermin seized Jasper. He kept his hands to his sides only with difficulty.

"That's only a start, Raferty. What I really wanna see is you eat dirt."

"What does that mean?"

"You think about it."

"You mean there's something I can do that will stop you?"

"I said all I'm gonna say."

The room seemed to be spinning as Jasper rasped, "But what about Asia? What about my daughter? You already hurt her—"

"At least you have a daughter...for now." He turned his back on the judge and banged on the door. When the guard opened it, he insisted, "Get me outta here! This place stinks with him in it."

Jasper fell into the nearest chair, the breath knocked out of him. He should have known that Crawley wouldn't be satisfied with Asia's attack. He meant to have her killed.

Burying his face in his hands, he tried to stifle his sobs. Asia would die because of him unless he did something to stop it. Eat dirt. That's what Crawley had said. But what the hell had that meant?

He couldn't think.

He could hardly breathe.

But somehow, someway, he had to stop Crawley, had to keep his daughter safe temporarily until he could think of a permanent way to stop the man.

He couldn't fathom why Asia had gone off on a goose chase after a dead woman, and with Crawley's son of all people! What could she have been thinking of?

Dakota had said she would be heading for the peninsula. He had to get someone after her. Fast. He thought about hiring a private detective, but that might take too long. Asia needed protection as soon as possible. Besides, someone more qualified came to mind. Someone who owed him a favor. An ex-con gone straight, who lived in Port Angeles, not all that far from Eagle Creek.

What better person to find his daughter and protect her? Jasper thought, his spirits rising. An ex-con was clever and tough and knew the criminal mind. Who better to ferret out danger? Yes, he had the perfect bodyguard for Asia.

With renewed hope that his daughter might live, Jasper rose from the table and left the dank room to place his call.

Chapter Four

"We're almost there," Asia said with rising excitement.

She checked the road map for at least the tenth time since leaving Port Angeles, where they'd had an early lunch. At the western side of the Olympic Peninsula, they were driving through timber country.

"I'd say another quarter of an hour." When Dominic merely grunted and kept his face turned to the road, she added, "Don't be so enthusiastic."

"I might if I thought Eagle Creek was going to be the solution to your problem."

"Maybe it will be."

"And maybe not," he countered, his tone realistic rather than overtly negative. "Even if we find Peggy Shield, what's to say she'll tell us where Jess is? My sister wouldn't have trusted just anyone. She's been carefully hiding herself for two years."

He had a point, not that Asia wanted to concede it. Ever hopeful, she planned to proceed with her usual assurance that if something could be done about a situation, she would manage it. Obviously Dominic had no such confidence.

"Do you ever take a positive attitude about anything?" she couldn't help asking.

He gave her a quick dark look. "What are we doing? Playing junior psychologist?"

"I'm merely trying to understand where you're coming from."

"You know where I come from."

She ignored the grim tone and continued. "I don't mean who your family is. I'm interested in you yourself. Don't you have some sense of personal identity that sets you apart from your father?"

"If I didn't, I wouldn't have gotten anywhere in the business world, which I did in spite of him." Now he was sounding downright defensive. "I was senior vice president of Peninsula Financial Consultants when his trial started."

And Dominic had been asked to resign from that position as soon as his own identity had been revealed, as Asia knew from her conversation with Dakota. That must have been awful for him, yet she couldn't understand why he hadn't fought back, gotten an even better job instead of caving in to the scandal sheets.

"Sounds like you're stuck in the past."

She noted his reaction to the accusation. His fingers gripped the steering wheel as if they might choke it...or was he thinking of her neck?

"Maybe I am," he said. "Something wrong with that?"

"With giving up? I'd say so." Asia was truly appalled at the thought—something she'd never do. "Where did quitting ever get anyone?"

"Where?" he echoed. "How about some peace of mind?"

"Do you really have peace of mind working on a ferry?"

His growled "Yes!" didn't sound convincing. "And there's nothing wrong with manual labor."

"I didn't say there was...unless it's the last thing in the world you want to do, and you're capable of more but you've just chucked it all."

She could tell she'd struck a sensitive chord. His cheek muscles tightened. But if she thought he was ready to retreat, she was wrong.

"Did anyone ever tell you you're annoying as hell?"

"Lots of people," Asia admitted, "starting with my family." She could have sworn he almost smiled at that.

"So, Miss Junior Psychologist, what about you?" he asked, smoothly turning the tables on her. "Are you always so perky?"

"I am not perky."

She tried not to be offended by the connotation, which she considered wishy-washy if not downright obnoxious...and not at all descriptive of her.

"All right. Disgustingly positive, then."

"I do my best."

"And what happens when you don't get what you want?"

Asia shrugged. "I don't know."

"That's a cop-out—"

"No," she interrupted, "it's not. I told you that I don't give up until I succeed."

He glanced away from the road long enough to give her an assessing look. "You pester people to death until they do anything to get you off their backs, right?"

Asia sank back in silence and stared out at the forested land, her eyes suddenly filling. Considering what hung in the balance between their success or failure, she considered his comment deliberately cruel.

Did refusing to give in to the likes of King Crawley really make her a pest?

"I'm sorry," he muttered as if he sensed her hurt. "That was uncalled for. I got carried away."

Asia slid him a glance. He seemed well-enough chagrined. She blinked away the threat of tears but didn't pick up on the conversation. She'd pushed him far enough. If she had one fault she'd admit to, he'd found it, right off. She sometimes drove people nuts because of her perseverance.

Of course, she assured herself in an effort to console, her tenacity was also her strength.

Even so, she couldn't help wondering if that trait was going to be her undoing this time. She'd forced Dominic into helping her, but though he claimed he wanted to do the right thing, she didn't know how far she could trust him. Protective of her own family, she realized a Raferty had no business trusting a Crawley, not even one who'd changed his name.

So why did she want to trust him so much that it hurt when he leveled his sarcasm at her?

Unwilling to explore the question further, Asia thought the turnoff to Eagle Creek didn't come too soon.

The first sense she had of the town's distress came when she spotted the former motel, a corner of which was burned, the rest boarded up. The town proper was small—several blocks in either direction—and had seen better days. Many buildings needed repair. Others were empty, hollow shells waiting for nature to sweep them away.

Asia knew the independent sawmill had been closed for more than a decade. With the main source of the town's income gone, she wondered how the remaining citizens of Eagle Creek made a living.

Dominic pulled up and parked in front of the small post office. Jumping down from her seat in the Bronco, Asia led the way inside.

"Afternoon!" she called cheerfully, putting on her best—if false—smile.

The single employee looked up, his expression carefully blank. "What can I do for you?"

As the door behind them creaked open once more, Dominic began, "We're looking for someone—"

But Asia interrupted. "We're looking for my sister. Her name is Peggy Shield." When the man didn't respond, she poked Dominic in the ribs. "Show him the letter, honey."

Dominic gave her a black look but pulled the folded envelope from his jeans pocket. Asia took it from him and offered it to the clerk.

"See." She tapped the faint red marking with a long, unpolished nail. "There's your Eagle Creek postmark, but no return address."

"Maybe your sister would have told you where she was if she wanted you to know."

"Oh, come on." Asia smiled rather convincingly under the man's narrow gaze. "She never expected me to come visit."

But he was still reluctant. "I don't know..."

"This is a small town. Someone's bound to tell us if you don't."

The man gave the envelope another once-over. "Olive Crawley, huh?" he said, reading the typewritten name. "If you're this Peggy's sister, then how come her last name isn't the same as yours?"

Asia said the first thing that came to her mind. "I'm married, of course. Shield was my maiden name. This is my husband, Dominic." Though she felt the man in question stiffening next to her, she ignored his reaction and hoped the clerk did likewise. "Peggy is going to be so happy when she sees us. We wanted to surprise her."

"Huh." Handing her the envelope, the clerk finally gave in. "I guess you'll find out anyhow. Check Miss Odel's Boarding House. Down the street and to the right. It's the big red building at the end of the block."

"Thanks."

But the clerk had already turned his attention to the person who had followed them inside. "Next."

With a fierce grip on her upper arm, Dominic swung Asia out of the post office, but not before she got a glimpse of the other patron, a grimy-looking man wearing jeans, a plaid shirt and a brimmed straw hat pulled low over his eyes. She got the distinct feeling that, while he wasn't looking directly at her, he was as aware of her as she was of him.

Maybe that's why she wasn't focused on the way Dominic was handling her until they reached the Bronco.

"Hey, let go," she protested, pulling her arm free.

The feeling that shook her stomach was odd, not at all the same reaction she'd had when he'd tried to take her arm that morning. And neither was he as conciliatory.

"Get in."

Though Dominic opened the door in a gentlemanly fashion, his tone was steel, and Asia didn't see any advantage in opposing him. She climbed into the passenger seat and made herself comfortable. Staying that way was difficult, however, when he seemed to be staring daggers at her. He waited until he'd pulled the four-wheeler away from the curb before sharing what was on his mind.

"That was quite a little performance you put on in there."

"Thanks," she said, even knowing he hadn't meant it as a compliment.

"But I'd like to be consulted before I'm introduced as anyone's husband," he went on.

"For Pete's sake! You'd think I was trying to commit you. It was the first thing that came to mind."

He grunted at that.

"And I intend to use the same story again if necessary," she asserted, "so consider yourself consulted."

"Now wait a minute—"

"Do you want to raise people's suspicions when it's not necessary?"

"All right, you've got a point."

To her relief, he dropped the subject. And a minute later, they left the vehicle in front of Miss Odel's Boarding House, one of the few places in town that had been kept up to former standards. The red paint and white trim were in good condition if not exactly fresh, and a riot of flowers lined the big white porch that half circled the old building.

The sixtyish woman who answered the door was as colorful as her setting. Her unnaturally dyed coal-black hair was curled tight and tied up with a turquoise scarf that matched her feather-trimmed, ankle-length kimono. Plastic orange earrings dangled from her lobes.

"Are you Miss Odel?" Asia asked.

"That I am. If you two are looking for a room, you'd best be married," the woman stated, orange- and purple-shadowed eyelids lowering in suspicion over bright blue eyes.

Giving Dominic an I-told-you-so expression was the highlight of Asia's afternoon. Not exactly having slept the night before, she was tiring fast and didn't protest when he took over.

"We're looking for Peggy Shield," Dominic said.

"She don't live here no more."

The woman was about to close the door in their faces when Dominic stuck out a large hand and stayed her. "Excuse me, can we come in?"

"What for?"

"We'd like to ask you about Peggy," Asia piped in.

"My wife's sister."

"You can do that right where you are."

"The sun is awfully strong," Dominic protested. And then, in a confidential tone, he added, "The little woman is pregnant." When Asia made a choked sound, he expertly covered. "She's still a little embarrassed by the good news. That's why we're looking for Peggy—to tell her in person."

Miss Odel gave an exaggerated sigh. "Oh, what the hay. Come on in."

"Thanks," Dominic said, placing a light hand between Asia's shoulder blades as he escorted her through the door into the old-fashioned living room. "Don't worry, sweetheart, you'll be fine as soon as you sit and have something cool to drink." He gave Miss Odel a pleading look. "That wouldn't be too much trouble, would it?"

"No, I guess not." Her orange earrings bounced along her shoulders as she shook her head. "Sit yourselves down and I'll be right back."

No sooner had the woman shuffled her turquoise mules through a swinging door in the long, formal dining room, than Asia whispered, "Pregnant?"

Dominic's green eyes mocked her. "It was the first thing that came to mind."

"I guess I deserved that."

And if she wasn't so tired, Asia knew she would laugh. Instead she leaned back against the couch, a fifties monstrosity in a pebbled mauve material. She barely had the strength to look around. The room was comfortable if in questionable taste, with garish knickknacks taking every available space. An ancient television blared an afternoon soap opera from across the room.

"Are you all right?"

Surprised, Asia met Dominic's concerned expression. "I'm pooped, but I'll get through this."

"You should have had something more substantial than a salad for lunch."

Her stomach was a bit hollow. "My appetite deserted me after last night."

The reminder of why they were there sobered Asia, made her realize how their pretense about their being married and her being pregnant seemed silly by comparison.

As though he was privy to her dark thoughts, Dominic said, "Asia, I really am sorry about what happened to you."

"It wasn't your fault."

"Maybe not."

Asia frowned and stared at the man. Dominic stood near the windows, profile to her. His expression was odd—could it possibly be guilt? Surely not. For all her ranting about how he should have stood up to his father rather than run away, he couldn't have done anything to slake the racketeer's thirst for vengeance.

Before she could figure out how to reassure him of that fact, Miss Odel came shuffling back into the room.

"Nothing like fresh lemonade to cure the vapors." The woman held out the glass to Asia. "Here you go—what did you say your name was?"

Giving Dominic a quick warning look, Asia took a sip and answered, "Olive Crawley," just in case she had to show the postmarked envelope again.

Miss Odel turned to him also. "And you're..."

"Dominic."

"Dominic Crawley." Her forehead puckered. "Name sounds familiar."

Asia was aware of the sudden tension that filled the room as Dominic went on edge, his body and expression tight. She immediately changed the subject before the landlady could pursue that line of thought.

"Miss Odel, when exactly did my sister move out?"

Though her forehead cleared, a pinched look around the woman's mouth clearly stated her disapproval when she said, "Late last week. Just up and went, and me with no notice, mind you. Left her room a mess." She sniffed indignantly. "I still haven't had time to clean up after her."

"Do you know where Peggy went?" Asia asked.

"Do I look like a social worker? I mind my own business. I have a policy of no interference with my boarders."

"Oh, dear, we've come all this way for nothing," Asia wailed, putting her distress on thick. She set down the glass. "Her room. Could we look at it?" She gave the landlady a hopeful expression. "If you haven't cleaned it up yet, maybe we can find something to tell us where she's gone."

"Be my guests." A crafty expression settled over Miss Odel's heavily made-up features. "As long as you're willing to pay, you can search the room to your heart's content."

"How much?" Dominic asked.

"I charge a hundred a week for the third-floor suite. That includes breakfast."

"We don't need the room for a week," Dominic countered. "Today will do. How about twenty?"

"Make it fifty and you got yourself a deal."

"Forty."

"Done."

"If you'll show us to—"

"In advance."

Dominic paid the woman, who then led the way to the third floor. Asia was feeling shaky by the time they climbed all those stairs and entered Peggy's former quarters. Far from a suite, the large room did have a love seat, as well as a small table and two padded chairs between the set of tall windows. The furniture was even older than that found in the living room. Asia's entire body yearned for the softness of the bed whose covers were rumpled and pulled back as if Peggy had slept there the night before. A few items strewn along the mirrored dresser reinforced that impression.

Unconsciously she stretched and smoothed the fall of hair from her face.

Miss Odel's eyes widened, and Asia realized the woman was staring at the side of her face that was bruised. She opened her coral mouth as if she were going to comment. Then, as if thinking better of breaking her no-interference policy, snapped her mouth shut. But she did give Dominic a dark look that made Asia twinge and smooth the hair back in place. Obviously the landlady thought he was responsible.

"One minute," Miss Odel said stiffly, leaving the room without closing the door. She opened another across the hall and pulled out a fresh set of sheets and towels. "You're lucky." She reentered the room, smiling directly at Asia. Setting down the linens on the edge of the unmade bed, she opened one of the two other doors in the room. "You have a private bath. The other two boarders on this floor share."

About to protest they weren't planning on staying, Asia was beaten to the punch by Dominic saying, "Thank you, Miss Odel. We'll be sure to find you if we need anything."

Handing him a ring with two keys, she gave him a sour look and straightened the feathers on her kimono sleeves. "Not until later, you won't. I don't like being disturbed when I watch my soaps."

"Later, then." He closed the door behind the landlady with a large sigh. "Alone at last."

Asia started at the possible double meaning, but told herself Dominic was referring to the opportunity to search the room. "Why don't you look through the bathroom while I work in here?"

"The load's a little uneven, don't you think? This is a pretty large room."

One she'd be more comfortable in alone at the moment. "You can help me when you're done in there."

His dark brows shot up at her tone, which was definitely cranky, but he didn't comment, merely went into the other room as she suggested. Asia sighed with relief. Dominic was such a forceful presence she found it restful to be away from him for a few moments.

She looked over the items scattered across the top of the dresser, but found nothing more significant than some crumpled if unused tissues, an empty Diet Coke can, an earring back and an almost-empty bottle of violet nail polish. The drawers themselves were empty.

Crossing the room, Asia sat on the edge of the bed and inspected the nightstand. Other than a Bible and a blank pad of paper and a pencil, the single drawer was empty. On the stand proper sat a cigarette pack, which she picked up and checked halfheartedly. Almost empty. The clear rectangle surrounded by a sea of dust on the top surface told her the pack had lain there for at least the week Miss Odel had claimed Peggy had been gone. She dropped the cigarettes back in place.

On the foot of the nightstand, newspapers and magazines were strewn haphazardly. She would look at them next, but in a moment. Meanwhile she would give in to temptation, which overwhelmed her. She lay back, thinking to rest long enough to get a second wind.

Exhaustion waylaid her good intentions as her head hit the pillow and she went out like a light.

DOMINIC SNAPPED OFF the bathroom light. Nothing in the medicine chest but a cardboard box with two Band-Aids, an almost empty bottle of mouthwash and a used razor. A toothbrush had been left on the sink, a magazine on the back of the toilet, a couple of used towels on the floor.

But no clues as to where this Peggy might have gone.

As he reentered the bedroom, he realized Asia hadn't found anything, either. As a matter of fact, she was curled in a fetal position on the bed, sound asleep.

About to continue his search alone, Dominic stopped. Noise would wake her, and he had the distinct feeling she could use a nap. He wondered if she'd slept at all the night before. She looked so peaceful... and vulnerable.

Her silvery hair had fallen away from the bruises that stood in stark contrast to her pale face. The Southwestern scarf puckered around her neck, revealing smudges he guessed to have been made by cruel fingers. And he could see a distinct nick under her jaw through the clear bandage.

His father's handiwork, Dominic thought, a bout of depression stripping him of his defenses, dropping him into the love seat where he sat and stared at the now-defenseless woman. He felt sick to his stomach.

How could the man who raised him, who had been so loving a parent, have done this?

Asia wasn't even King Crawley's enemy. That was the worst part, the part that didn't make sense, not even for a man who had a very different set of ethics from his son. His father had taken to punishing innocents. He really had become warped to stoop so low.

Dominic threw back his head, passed a hand over his face, wished he could so easily wipe away the guilt that nagged at him. If he had fought his father on his own ground instead of running away to prove himself, could he have prevented this obscenity? And what about other tragedies?

The burden of his father's crimes pressed down on his shoulders.

He tried to clear his head, to stop tormenting himself for what he couldn't change, but the mind was a powerful weapon. It punished him not for what he had done, but for what he hadn't stopped.

He sat and let his thoughts wander and go where they would until he fell into a stupor. And then he must have dozed for a while. The next thing he knew, he seemed to be coming out of a trance, his quiet disturbed by the sounds of Asia moving around in the bed, making noises deep in her throat as if she were frightened.

Dominic flew from the love seat to stand over her. Still asleep, she was undoubtedly having a nightmare. Her face was pulled into a mask of terror and she was trembling, moving restlessly over the mattress as if trying to get away from danger. The soft cry that came from deep within her made the hair on his arms stand up.

"Asia," he crooned softly, instinct making him want to take her in his arms. He sat at the edge of the bed but didn't touch her. "It's all right. No one is going to hurt you."

Her expression changed as though his voice pierced her subconscious.

And then hoarse words escaped her lips. "No, don't. Please." Her head thrashed on the pillow, sending the silver threads of her hair in every direction.

"Asia..."

He thought about waking her, but sleep was obviously what she needed most. Sleep undisturbed by visions that were more than dreams, that were all-too-real memories. Without consciously thinking about what he was doing, Dominic smoothed the hair from her face, gentled her with a soft touch and even softer, if meaningless, words.

Sighing, she finally settled down, her expression clearing, her body relaxing at last. And in her sleep, she found him as he was withdrawing, her hand lightly trapping his on the pillow. Dominic felt an odd, foreign emotion course through him, and he sat there frozen, unable to move, unable to extricate his hand from hers.

An invisible bond tethered him to her, though he knew if Asia were awake she would abhor his touch. And how could he blame her? After what she'd been through, she'd reject any man's touch right now. Definitely his. And with as much certainty, he knew that he wanted to do more than hold her hand. She was a striking woman, one who appealed to all the senses.

One who stirred him as no other had done before, he thought, finding the fact ironic. She'd made him face years of repressed guilt.

And that was why he would never be able to do more than innocently touch her. Guilt. Asia was a Raferty, and even if he had changed his name, Dominic was still a Crawley. Oil and water didn't mix.

Still, he could touch her now, while she was still unaware of his presence. He didn't move for what must have been an hour, before she finally rolled over and stretched, clearly in the throes of waking. Slipping from the bed with care so as not to alert her, Dominic froze when her eyes opened and she saw him standing over her.

"What..."

"You fell asleep," he said. The glimmer of panic in her gaze, he covered by picking up the cigarettes from the nightstand. "I got tired of waiting for you to wake, so I decided to search in here anyway."

She pushed herself up and away from him, ran a shaky hand through her hair, then checked her watch. "You must have waited for quite a while. It's after six."

Her voice was husky. Sexy. Making him too aware of her.

Dominic shrugged. "I slept, too," he admitted, then to soothe her wide-eyed expression explained, "on the love seat."

"Oh."

Asia climbed out of bed on the side opposite him. Still not fully awake, she seemed disoriented, and for once, unsure of herself. Dominic forced himself to look away from her and down at the cigarettes. He turned the pack. Under the cellophane lay a book of matches.

"Did you find anything?" she asked.

"Afraid not. But I haven't finished looking."

"Sorry." Embarrassment stained her otherwise pale face. "My fault."

"None of this is your fault."

Asia glanced at a chest of drawers a few feet away. "I'll go through these drawers," she muttered.

Dominic dropped the cigarettes onto the night-stand. "Did you get a chance to check the closet?"

She shook her head. Then they both got busy. Neither came up with a thing. She plopped down on the side of the bed and began going through the reading material strewn at its base. He looked under furniture, dressers, the bed, and found exactly one crumpled tissue and a balled up pair of panty hose.

"Both local and Seattle newspapers here," Asia said, sounding disappointed. "Nothing to tell us where Peggy went." She dropped the pile back into place. "So, what now?"

Dominic's stomach growled in answer. "Eat. You are hungry, right?"

"Yes, but—"

"Food will replenish starving brain cells."

"And we can ask about Peggy." Asia rose as Dominic got to her. "Surely other people in town knew her. Maybe she had a favorite place."

"I don't think there are too many in town to choose from." Then Dominic remembered the matches. "I've got it!" He picked up the pack of cigarettes and checked out the matches. Red lettering advertised a local bar. "If we find out anything about our mystery woman, it'll probably be at Tully's Tap and Grill."

Chapter Five

"Do you want to approach the bartender or should I?" Asia asked as they entered the dark, worn-looking establishment barely a half hour later.

"Let's play this cautiously," Dominic suggested. "Order food first."

That he was steering her past the bar with its half dozen customers, his large hand square in the middle of her back, didn't bother Asia—she was getting used to his habit of touching her in that polite manner. The idea of waiting to ask questions, however, made her anxious and quick to object.

"But—"

"We don't want to raise suspicions, right?"

"We can use the same story—"

"Later," Dominic growled, his tone brooking no argument as he stopped at one of four empty Formica-topped tables surrounding the old-fashioned jukebox.

With an exasperated sigh, Asia sat in a rickety chair, her gaze never leaving the man who sprawled next to her. "Did anyone ever tell you you're annoying as hell?" she asked, reiterating his own words to her earlier.

Dominic's sensual mouth pulled into an easy grin that startled her. He was usually taut as a bowstring—his anger always seeming to simmer below the surface—and just as defensive.

"I'll let you be the first," he said.

"Right."

"Have a menu."

He handed her a greasy blue page, which he took from between the napkin rack and a bottle of catsup.

Irritation pulled at Asia, competing with an attraction she wished she could deny. She didn't want to be interested in any man, especially not Dominic Crawford. They were allies with a common goal. And she'd had to shame him into helping her at that, a fact she could hardly forget.

Neither could she forget the dream she'd had. What started as a nightmare with her struggling against the unknown attacker all over again had ended as a disturbing memory. She'd imagined Dominic calming her with gentle words and touch. Within his sphere, she'd felt so safe . . .

Until she'd awakened, that was.

Then the danger of her situation had come crashing back down on her. She'd even reexamined her thinking while she helped search the room. Was she crazy for joining forces with the devil's spawn?

"So, do you want a cheeseburger and fries?"

Asia realized she'd been staring at the limited menu without really seeing it. Now that she looked, she saw six variations of the all-American meal.

"Sure," she said, sticking the blue paper back in place.

Dominic signaled the man behind the bar. "Two double cheeseburgers and fries. And two beers." After the fact, he said, "You do drink beer, don't you?"

"Sometimes."

Then she was annoyed when he didn't bother to follow that up by asking her if she wanted something else *this* time. His look of amusement didn't sit well, either.

"Are you always so feisty?" he asked.

"What?"

"I have the feeling that you came into the world ready for battle."

"Something wrong with that?"

"Not at all. It's just an observation. It says something for the way you were raised."

"That's how much you know," she said, relaxing despite herself. "My parents were never exactly thrilled with my independent nature."

"Neither were mine."

Because she didn't know how to respond to that, considering she'd already expressed her disapproval of his life's choice to take a road that led away from his family, Asia kept the conversation on herself.

"As a matter of fact," she said, "my parents thought I was a stubborn brat and far too daring for my own good."

Dominic's expression told her he agreed. "Obviously their opinions didn't affect you."

"Well, they didn't make me change." But it had hurt that she'd been at odds with her family so often.

"You always did as you pleased?"

"Usually. Like before my senior year in college, I took off for Europe and hitched around the Continent with two fellow students. We stayed in hostels and pensions and ate at little holes-in-the-wall that catered to the locals. My family was horrified, especially my father. He figured that if I didn't get mugged, I would come down with some horrible disease from unsanitary conditions.''

Dominic laughed. ''I'd say that took a lot of guts for a girl who could probably have afforded a more conventional way of seeing Europe.''

''Sure. I could have taken an escorted tour. My father would have paid anything to keep me 'safe.'''

''You don't like being safe?''

''Not using the conventional definition. I was born to take risks. I get bored if things go too smoothly,'' Asia admitted, thinking of her penchant for leaving her business from time to time and wandering. ''My parents figured I associated with the wrong crowd, but they were off base. I've just been in touch with this daring part of me ever since I can remember.'' She thought of her current situation and was quick to add, ''Not that I like the kind of danger...''

Asia stopped before she added *that your father put me in*. Dominic got the message. His features tightened, though not in anger. She didn't know what to say to breach the awkward silence.

''Two beers, burgers coming up.''

Identical mugs were slapped down on the table by the bartender, a big man wearing an apron that would never see white again. At least he looked friendly enough, with an open expression and a smile softening thick lips under a full salt-and-pepper mustache.

''Is this your place?'' Dominic asked.

''Yeah, I'm Tully. You folks are new in town.''

''Just passing through. We actually came this way to look someone up. Peggy Shield. You know her?''

"Sure, I know the kid." Tully's smile broadened to show off a dimple in his fleshy cheek. "Used to come in here regular. Haven't seen her in a while, though."

"Peggy was staying at Miss Odel's," Asia said. "She moved last week. We're trying to figure out where she might have gone. I'm her sister."

"Sister? You don't look nothing alike."

Asia was trying to decide if she should say they were only half sisters when he went on.

"'Course that don't mean nothing these days. You females are always changing your hair color or makeup and such." He gave Asia a broad wink, which made her think he suspected she bleached her hair. "Sometimes a man has to look hard to see the real woman. Maybe someone finally did. Maybe Peggy found a boyfriend who took her away from Eagle Creek," he clarified. "I was always teasing her 'cause she wouldn't give the men who came in here the time of day."

"I never thought of a boyfriend," Asia admitted. If Peggy had found a man, would that make their search harder? "Is there anyone around here who might know for sure?"

He shrugged. "Maybe Marcie Lem. They were friendly, you know."

"Where can we find this Marcie?"

"Hey, Tully, you ever gonna stop jawin'?" a man at the bar complained loudly. "I need another whiskey."

"Hold on to your pants, Biff." Turning back to Asia, he said, "You'll find Marcie here, most likely. She usually comes in a little after nine, when the drugstore closes."

"Maybe we'll wait around for her."

"You do that," Tully said, backing away as Biff threatened to jump the bar and get his own whiskey. "I can use all the customers I can get."

When the big man was out of hearing range, Asia said, "He's a friendly sort. A nice change from the suspicious Miss Odel. If you hadn't paid her, that woman wouldn't have given us the time of day." Remembering Dominic had lost his job because he chose to help her, she realized he couldn't afford extra expenses. She reached for the shoulder bag she'd hung over the back of the chair. "Speaking of money, I'll give you the forty and pay for dinner."

He stayed her hand. "That's not necessary."

"But I want to."

"All right. Pay for dinner then."

Nodding in agreement, she let go of the bag and wondered how she was going to manage giving him back his money. "And for somewhere to stay tonight."

"We have a place. Miss Odel's."

"Right. One room." And one bed, she added silently. "We can't exactly ask her for another after the story we gave her."

"And I don't think we'd have much success trying to get accommodations at that burned-out motel we passed."

"There are other towns."

"Not many in this area. And by the time we find this Marcie and talk to her, who knows how late it'll be." There wasn't a hint of amusement in his expression when he said, "If you're thinking about there being only one bed in the room at Miss Odel's, you can have it all to yourself. I'll take the couch."

"It's a love seat," she argued, "and far too small for you. If anyone sleeps there, it should be me."

"If you insist."

Asia realized she'd just been railroaded, had committed herself to sharing a room with a man who was a stranger, one who could be dangerous. Less than twenty-four hours before, a man had attacked her with the intention of raping her. He'd touched her everywhere, and all the scrubbing in the world wasn't going to erase the invisible imprint of his hands. She shuddered at the memory.

But looking at Dominic, who sat back in his chair waiting for her decision with a purposely blank expression, Asia realized she wasn't in the least afraid.

DOMINIC NOTICED the attractive little brunette the moment she walked in the door. As did every other man in the place.

"Hiya, Marcie," a sandy-haired guy at the bar called. "Buy you a drink?"

"Sure, Sam." Glancing over at Tully she said, "My usual," then slid onto the stool next to the man.

"Gotcha."

Dominic realized Asia was gripping his arm. "There she is," she whispered excitedly. "How do you want to approach her?"

Startled, Dominic pulled back. "Me? You're asking for my opinion now?"

As if suddenly realizing she was hanging on to him unnecessarily, Asia let go. "So I'm a little strung out from all this waiting."

"Just stick to the story."

Tully was setting down what looked like a seltzer with a twist of lime in front of the woman. "Got a coupla folks who want to talk to you,'' the bartender said, pointing in their direction. ''About Peggy Shield.''

The brunette glanced over her shoulder and raised her brows. She looked none too friendly as she asked, ''Yeah, what about Peg?''

That was their cue. Dominic rose and indicated Asia should do the same. He picked up the beers they'd been nursing for the past hour and carried them over to the bar where he set them down. Though the place had pretty much filled up since they'd arrived, an empty stool remained next to Marcie. He held it out for Asia.

''I'm Peggy's sister.'' Asia slid onto the seat and smiled at the other woman. ''She didn't tell us she was mov—''

''Peggy didn't have any sister.''

Asia's mouth dropped open. Dominic put a steadying hand on her shoulder.

''She told you that?'' he demanded to know.

''Don't use that tone with the lady,'' the sandy-haired man on Marcie's other side ordered.

''It's all right, Sam.'' Marcie took a sip of her drink before answering. ''No, she didn't tell me in so many words.''

''Then why would you say such a horrible thing to me?'' Asia asked.

What a little actress. If Dominic didn't know better, he would swear Asia was hurt.

''I got to know Peg pretty well, better'n anyone in town,'' Marcie stated. ''She mentioned her brother a few times—and how much she missed him—but never a sister.''

Dominic could practically hear the wheels spinning in Asia's head as she said, "Oh, I see. So she was still angry even though she wrote me." At the other woman's questioning look, she explained, "We had a major disagreement."

Asia found and gripped Dominic's hand so hard he thought she might break it. Sensing she was trying to prepare him for something, he wondered what her fertile imagination had come up with now.

"You had a fight, so she pretended you didn't exist?" Marcie looked disbelieving. "Over what?"

Her expression odd, Asia glanced up at Dominic. "Over him."

"A man?"

"Who is now my husband." Asia hung her head sheepishly. "I'm afraid I stole my sister's boyfriend. Peggy couldn't stand losing him, so she took off."

Dominic couldn't believe how their fictitious relationship was growing. And Marcie wasn't the only one interested in it. On the other side of the bar, a man who looked vaguely familiar stared at them from beneath his brimmed straw hat.

"We thought it was time we all made peace," Dominic said, looking back to the brunette. When he realized she was glaring at him angrily, he added, "Especially since Peggy's going to be an aunt."

This time Marcie's mouth dropped open. She took another sip of her selzer and seemed to be mulling over their story. Finally she made up her mind to believe them.

"So what's your name?" she asked.

"Olive."

A glint of recognition lighted Marcie's dark eyes. "I remember her mailing a letter to an Olive in Seattle."

Asia nodded eagerly. "Me."

"Okay, so maybe you are her sister."

Dominic felt Asia sag in relief against him. "Then you'll help us find her?" he asked.

Marcie shrugged. "I might if I knew where she went."

"Oh, no!" This time, Asia's protest had the ring of sincerity. She grabbed her beer and took a gulp. "We've got to find her. Don't you have any idea of where she might be?"

"All I know is she got a job at some lumber company," Marcie said grudgingly.

"She didn't mention the company's name?" Dominic asked.

Giving him an appraising look, Marcie shook her head. "If she did, I don't remember."

Dominic guessed she didn't want to remember, that all her suspicions weren't appeased. He sensed she knew more than she was saying, was already regretting telling them anything at all. They weren't able to get anything more specific out of the woman.

"Maybe we should leave, hon," Dominic finally said, squeezing Asia's shoulders. "You know you need your rest."

"He's right." Marcie indicated Asia's beer. "And you shouldn't be drinking. It's not good for the baby."

With a guilty start, Asia slammed the beer mug on the bar. "Guess I wasn't thinking straight."

Once they were back on the street and on their way to Miss Odel's a few minutes later, Dominic thought it ironic that they could be so convincing that Marcie worried about some fictitious baby even while covering up for Peggy. If they weren't careful, their lies would get them in hot water yet. Keeping up the pretense would undoubtedly get harder, and they would start mixing up the pieces of their story.

A furtive movement from the corner of his eye made Dominic whip his head around to check the street behind them. All he saw was a dark shape meld with the shadows of a storefront. His heartbeat steadied. A local returning home, that was all. He was too imaginative. No one could possibly be following them. No one knew where they'd headed.

Asia's sigh returned his attention to her. "Do you think we're on a wild goose chase?" she asked.

Not having heard her sound so unsure of herself before, Dominic was surprised by the question. "Maybe."

"You warned me it wasn't going to be so easy. If you said 'I told you so' and wanted to go home and forget you ever met me, I wouldn't blame you."

Dominic knew he would never forget Asia Raferty. Not that he wanted to try. Whether he wanted to or not, he was getting attached to the willowy blonde. He couldn't stand the idea of discouraging her. Abandoning her was out of the question. Besides, her positive attitude seemed to be catching. If for more complex reasons than her own, he wanted to find Jess as much as she did. And Peggy Shield seemed to be the only person who could lead them to his sister.

"We're in this together," Dominic assured Asia, once more glancing over his shoulder. Behind them, the street was deserted. Then Asia's relief washed over him like a soothing wave, stirring him oddly, making him give her his complete attention. "In the morning, we'll find out what lumber companies are working in this area."

"Maybe we won't have to wait till morning," Asia said as they crossed the street toward Miss Odel's. "Remember that pile of newspapers under the nightstand?"

He did, indeed. Stopping only to take her overnight bag and his duffel out of the Bronco, they hurried inside.

Once in their third-floor room, Asia grabbed the newspapers and dropped them on the bed. He sat next to her. First they went through the pile section by section, setting aside the want ads from the local papers. Done, they began scanning the Help Wanted columns.

Dominic had no luck, but within a few minutes, Asia cried, "Here it is! Listen." Her voice throbbed with excitement as she read. "'Mountain Timber Company needs workers in all abilities for commuter logging camp: loggers, drivers, office, KP.' That's the only logging company advertising for help."

For the first time since they'd started their strange journey together, Dominic really smelled success. "We'll call Mountain Timber first thing in the morning and..."

His words trailed off as he realized Asia was blinking rapidly as if trying to hide the moisture building in her eyes.

"Hey, what's wrong?" he asked softly. "I thought you'd be happy."

"I am happy." Seeming embarrassed by her show of emotion, she swallowed hard. "I just want you to know how much this means to me."

"Finding the want ad?"

She shook her head. "Your sticking with me. For all my brave talk, I don't know that I could do this alone."

"You won't have to. I promise."

The urge to take her in his arms was uncontrollable. She stiffened only for a second before relaxing against his chest. A protective feeling swelled through Dominic and he tightened his hold. That was obviously too much for Asia, who pushed herself out of his arms and popped up off the bed.

"I'll use the bathroom first." Color stained her cheeks as she picked up the overnight bag and a set of clean towels and hurried inside the bathroom. Through a half-open door she said, "And I was serious about my sleeping on the love seat, so don't get any ideas about confiscating it."

She shut the door swiftly.

The ordinary sounds issuing from the bathroom—water running, teeth being brushed—were oddly intimate. And as disturbing as the thought of sleeping on the same sheets the lovely woman had used earlier.

Dominic stripped them from the bed and slipped on the clean bottom sheet Miss Odel had provided. Asia could have the top sheet, one of the blankets and both pillows. He knew she was serious about his using the bed. Being obstinate about letting her have it wouldn't improve relations between them.

And Dominic knew he wanted that—comfortable relations with a woman he respected and was attracted to—for as long as possible. He understood that once they found Jess and settled the vendetta, Asia would be out of his life for good.

The realization made him feel hollow inside, as if part of him had been ripped out.

Ridiculous. He hardly knew the woman. He was merely lonely. He needed female companionship. Soft hair. Soft body. Groaning, Dominic ordered himself to knock off the fantasies. He would only succeed in torturing himself. Just because she'd allowed him to put his arms around her for a few seconds without jumping out of her skin didn't mean Asia had gotten over what happened to her.

Or that she'd want him, a Crawley.

By the time she exited the bathroom, he'd worked himself into a foul mood and merely grunted as Asia passed him. Stopping short, she stared at him in surprise. She wore a knee-length nightshirt in a lavender shade that made her hair seem more silver than blond. He firmly closed the door on what he couldn't have.

He saw a long night loom ahead. Though he was nearly exhausted and the bed seemed a comfortable one, he didn't think he was in for much sleep.

At least Asia would be safe with him. As long as he was around, nothing terrible would happen to her.

Dominic took comfort from that thought.

THE THIRD-FLOOR ROOM of Miss Odel's Boarding House went dark. And the person watching from the opposite side of the street sagged in relief. As luck would have it, they weren't going anywhere tonight.

Tomorrow was another day...one that would undoubtedly bring opportunities to get closer to the Raferty woman.

Finding her had been a snap. Following shouldn't be too difficult. The watcher climbed into a porch swing and settled down for a good night's sleep.

Chapter Six

Asia awoke practically at the crack of dawn. Fuzzy-headed, it took her a while to realize where she was. Then, heart hammering, she bolted upright in bed and slid away from the long bulge on the other side. But the lump proved to be no more than bunched covers.

Gazing around the room bathed in early-morning light, she noticed the love seat was empty, stripped of its cushions. They—and Dominic—were on the floor.

She sank to the edge of the mattress. She'd fallen asleep on the love seat to the sounds of Dominic's tossing and turning. Sometime during the night he must have picked her up and placed her on the bed, trading his comfort for hers.

But why?

She stared down at the strange man who didn't by any stretch of the imagination fit on two cushions. The bedsheet tangled his bare legs, thick with muscle and curly black hair. The long limbs hugged the chilly wooden floor. The night before, the room had been too dark to see what he'd worn to bed. Now she realized a pair of briefs was all that covered him.

Her mouth went dry and, before she knew what she was doing, she spent precious seconds staring at the line where white cotton met tanned flesh.

She started and flushed with embarrassment, scooted back onto the bed more fully, pulled the covers over her and tried to force herself back to sleep. She couldn't be attracted to Dominic, didn't want to be. Not to him, not to any man. At least not now, not so soon after her close escape. Her heart was pounding practically out of her chest, putting a lie to her wishes. She had no intellectual control over her baser instincts, had no control over who or when.

That Dominic was King Crawley's son didn't even seem to matter.

Thoughts of this tantalizing man, when added to the task before them, made sleep impossible. Tossing and turning to no avail, she finally gave up. They might as well be on their way as early as possible.

Asia arose and made enough noise to wake the dead as she performed her morning ablutions.

But Dominic was still asleep when she left the bathroom. She'd showered, done her hair and makeup, dressed in jeans and a sea-green T-shirt. She'd removed the tape over the cut, and the bruises were already fading, but she didn't want to explain anything to some curious stranger. Certain Miss Odel had assumed Dominic had hurt her, Asia had been mortified. She carefully tied a printed cotton kerchief around her neck.

She checked her watch. Far too early for breakfast. But she was ready to leave, and Dominic continued to sleep like a dead man. Figuring he might not have had much sleep, she didn't want to wake him.

So what to do?

Her nails were a mess. She used an emery board on the tips, then fetched the nearly empty bottle of polish she'd found on the dresser. The stuff was a little goopy, having thickened with exposure to air, but a single coat would do until she stopped at a drugstore where she could pick up some toiletries. Sitting cross-legged on the bed, she carefully brushed on the odd shade of violet enamel.

She was just finishing the hurried manicure when Dominic groaned and turned toward her on the cushions, his masculine features twisted.

"What's that nasty smell?"

"Nail polish." Unable to help herself, she shoved a hand practically in his face. If the potent smell didn't wake him up fully, nothing would. "Like it?"

Asia bit her lip so she wouldn't laugh at his expression. Not only was he trying not to breathe in the fumes, but he was eyeing the results with distaste.

"You really like that garish stuff?" he croaked, his voice early-morning gravelly. "Reminds me of the color polish Jess used to wear. She had a thing about wanting to be noticed."

Mulling that over as she withdrew her hand, Asia said, "It's not a shade I would have chosen. I found the bottle on the dresser."

Dominic furrowed his brow and stated, "That must mean Jess has been here!" He quickly rose from the cushions on the floor. He dragged the sheet with him but only half succeeded in covering himself more modestly. "Maybe she was visiting Peggy and left her nail polish behind."

Thinking that Peggy likely had the same taste in colors—a more logical explanation—Asia didn't voice the opinion. There was no reason to discourage Dominic, not when he was looking so hopeful. She didn't want to wipe the positive smile from his face. The foreign expression suited him, lightened features that could be heavy with menace when he was angry. Which seemed to be a good portion of the time, Asia knew. That she was becoming all too aware of his feelings disturbed her.

As did his state of undress, when she realized this almost-nude man was practically close enough for her to count the individual hairs on his well-muscled thigh if she so chose.

"Listen, I'm ready to go." Pulse erratic once more, she slipped off the bed and concentrated on replacing the bottle on the dresser so she wouldn't have to look at him. "Why don't you shower and dress. Then we can find someplace in town to have a good breakfast before we start out."

"What's the rush? It's probably too early to call Mountain Timber for directions anyway."

"It won't be by the time we finish eating. I'd just like to get going, okay?" she said, knowing she was being unreasonable. She grabbed her overnight bag and her purse, cleverly eluding having to face him. "If you give me the keys, I'll wait for you outside."

"If that'll make you happy." His words were clipped, his visage carefully blank. He found the key ring and threw it to her with a gruff "Catch."

Asia grabbed for the keys, which landed against her palm with a jangle. Her fingers closed around the cool metal and she turned away, feeling Dominic's eyes bore into her back as she left the room. The big house was quiet as she slipped down the stairs and out the front way. The street stood equally silent, the opening of the Bronco's door the only sound.

And yet something made her freeze as she made to get inside. That she felt exactly as she had just before she'd been attacked made her pulse race. Was it possible that she was being watched? Scrambling into the passenger seat, she locked the door and stared out through closed windows, giving the neighborhood a once-over. Nothing untoward caught her gaze.

And yet the uneasy feeling persisted.

Asia remained on guard until she began to feel foolish. What was her problem? First she'd overreacted to Dominic for no reason. That he was a magnificent male wasn't his fault. He hadn't been trying to provoke some reaction from her. She'd been far too sensitive where he was concerned.

And now this annoying feeling was gnawing at her. No one knew where she had gone except her own family. She was safe, Asia reassured herself. If only Dominic was here beside her, she might believe it.

The ten minutes it took him to clean up and join her seemed interminable. He threw his bag in back and climbed into the driver's seat as though nothing had happened, as though he didn't notice she was jittery, as though she hadn't behaved like an absolute idiot in their room.

And yet, she sensed an acerbic anger burning right below his surface.

If he noticed her looking around warily as he moved the four-wheeler away from Miss Odel's, he didn't comment, not until they were seated in a dive called Fanny's and were halfway through their first cup of coffee.

"Are you going to tell me what's wrong, or am I going to have to guess?" he asked, his tone cool.

Which did he mean—her reason for practically running from their room or the way she'd been looking over her shoulder since? She chose to answer the second.

"I, uh, have the weirdest feeling that someone was watching me while I was waiting for you."

His expression changed slightly, to one more concerned. "Did you see anyone?"

Asia shook her head. "Just nerves, I guess, now that we're getting so close."

Some of that pent-up anger seemed to smolder out of him and he visibly relaxed. "You did seem kind of jumpy this morning. I thought maybe you were regretting... things."

Like asking for his help? She wanted to reassure him that she trusted him, but some sense of self-preservation kept her from doing so. She was feeling too close to a man whose true loyalties lay elsewhere. Just as did hers. They didn't need some attraction confusing things. Better that they remain as distant as they'd begun.

"Everything about this situation makes me jumpy," she finally said, quickly turning to the door as it creaked open.

She relaxed when a woman with spiked red hair walked in and took a nearby seat at the counter, back to them.

Dominic was checking his watch. "I might as well try calling Mountain Timber."

His impersonal tone told her he'd received her message.

Going to the pay phone on the wall next to the counter, he pulled out a small pad of paper on which he'd written the number for Mountain Timber Company.

While Dominic was dialing, another customer entered, a tall, leanly muscled man in jeans and a T-shirt decorated with a fancy if faded cow skull. His brown eyes didn't seem to miss a thing. Asia swallowed hard as his gaze swept over her, resting on her for a second. Then he broke contact and signaled the waitress for a cup of coffee.

"I need directions to get to your lumber camp from Eagle Creek," Dominic was saying loud enough for her—or anyone else in the place—to hear.

He tore the top sheet from the pad and set it to the side, then began scribbling whatever information the person on the other end gave him.

"Then it's what, about an hour or so drive?" Dominic asked, replacing the pad and pen in his pocket.

Asia noticed something fall to the floor near his feet, but her attention was immediately diverted by the waitress bringing their plates of ham, eggs, hash browns and pancakes. She was unable to resist digging in without waiting for Dominic to rejoin her.

"You still have jobs available, right?" He paused a second for an answer before adding, "Great. We'll be there soon."

He hung up and seconds later slid back into their booth.

"Why did you ask whether or not there were jobs?" Asia asked.

"So we can get work." He lowered his voice. "We've been lucky about getting information so far, but the tall tale we've concocted is wearing thin. The loggers I've met are protective of their own. We go in there, questions blazing, and they'll clam up for sure. Peggy might not even be working at the commuter camp. She could be at some other location. But if we get jobs, we'll have a better chance of tracking her down.''

His explanation sounded sensible, and Asia was relieved that she didn't have to tell people she was Olive Crawley anymore. ''So how do we introduce ourselves?''

''Friends, traveling companions...any way you want it.''

Asia didn't like the idea of being too far from Dominic and wanted to ensure she'd feel safe by staying as close to him as possible at all times.

Hoping they could once more share accommodations—something more spacious than a single-bedded room for her peace of mind, she suggested, ''How about *good* friends?''

''As long as you're willing to make it believable.''

His challenge made her insides curl, but she wouldn't react as she had that morning. ''I'm willing to play my part. At least we'll be able to use our real names.''

Since his mouth was full, Dominic merely grunted in agreement. Asia spent the next few minutes eating most of her huge breakfast. As she and Dominic made small talk, she felt better than she had since she'd awakened.

Then Dominic brought the subject back to their venture. ''We'll have to stop for gas on the way out of town.'' He washed down a swallow of food with a long swig of coffee. ''I'll feel better if we have a full tank. Who knows when we'll find another gas station in this neck of the woods.''

Sudden movement from the corner of her eye prompted Asia to glance over her shoulder as the red-haired woman left with a friendly wave to the waitress. And to her surprise, she realized the man with the skull T-shirt was no longer sitting at the counter.

Dominic pulled out the pad of paper with directions and set it on the table, then seemed perturbed as he continued going through his pockets.

"Something wrong?"

"I must be absentminded this morning. I can't figure out where I put Mountain Timber's phone number."

"Maybe you dropped it by the telephone. I saw something fall."

Dominic quickly checked but slid back into the booth, shaking his head. "Oh, well, I don't suppose it really matters since we'll be at the camp soon."

Unable to eat another bite, Asia set down her fork and took a look at the directions. "Do you know all the roads around here?"

"No, but I have a pretty detailed map in the Bronco."

"Why don't you finish eating and I'll go get it. We can figure out how to get to the camp over coffee."

This time, he placed the keys in her hand.

When she walked out of Fanny's, Asia was surprised to see the town bustling with people and vehicles, though the hour was still early. Maneuvering around two cars parked too close together, she crossed the street to Dominic's truck and fetched the road map from his glove compartment.

Some distance away, an engine revved.

Asia registered the sound without thinking anything of it.

Unfolding the map, she started to cross back to the greasy spoon. The engine revved higher, and she realized the sound was coming her way. She looked down the street. A pickup truck was heading directly for her and closing fast. Startled, she faltered, almost tripping.

Then a burst of adrenaline automatically shot her legs forward toward the other side of the street. The oncoming vehicle seemed to swerve with her. The scene played itself out in slow motion to her frightened eyes. Her heart pumped as she sought an escape route. Knowing she couldn't run between the two cars parked practically nose to tail, she leaped for one of the bumpers and banged her thigh on the hood ornament as the truck sped by and careened down the street.

The car she stood on bounced under her, a countermeasure to the irregular beat of her heart. And her breath was coming in fits and spurts. She was trying to keep her balance, waiting for everything to steady before jumping down to the sidewalk.

"WHAT THE HELL is going on?" Dominic demanded, having slammed out of Fanny's after looking out the window and seeing Asia on top of the car.

She waved the map toward the end of the street. "Someone tried to run me down. Didn't you see?"

"I didn't have an unobstructed view of the window. All I saw was you up there." He gave her a hand and helped her down, was almost tempted to put a comforting arm around her. But she'd made it perfectly clear that she wanted to keep a friendly distance between them, so he let go of her instead. "What did the car look like?"

"A truck. A pickup. I—I didn't notice what kind or what color," she admitted, her face flushed with exertion. "I think it was light. Beige or tan."

As they reentered the restaurant, several people seemed interested in the drama. Dominic whisked Asia by their prying eyes and into their booth.

Then, in a low voice intended for her ears only, he asked, "You think someone was purposely trying to run you down?"

The color faded from her beautiful face, leaving in its place a sickly pallor. "I—I don't know."

"Maybe it was some drunk," he said in an effort to reassure her otherwise.

"At this time of the morning?"

"It's been known to happen." Though Dominic didn't believe this was an accident any more than she did. "You didn't get a look at the driver, did you?"

"Afraid not. I was too busy trying to keep from being a road kill."

Dominic couldn't smile at her attempt at humor. He picked up his fork and resumed eating, but the food was now cold and tasteless. He had another cup of coffee and traced their route into the Olympic National Forest for her instead. They had to go through the town of Olympia Grove, and on to a series of lumber roads cut through the forest as logging truck routes. Only the largest were marked on the map.

All the while he kept Asia occupied, a less involved part of him was mulling over what had just happened to her.

Had one of his father's men tracked her down? If only he'd seen what had happened.

And yet, would that have proved anything? Since he wasn't acquainted with many of the people working for the old man anymore, Dominic doubted he would know the person if they met face-to-face. Frustration threatened to darken his mood, yet he fought such an intrusion of his spirit, if not for his own sake, then for hers. She didn't need his brand of negative thinking. Neither did he, for that matter.

For too long he'd let himself be defeated by fates he'd decided he couldn't control. He'd have to try harder to take fate into his own hands. If he succeeded at nothing else, he would make certain Asia was safe. She'd been through enough because of his father. More than compassion for a victim, however, Dominic was feeling stronger emotions, ones he hadn't wanted to face.

And he'd already realized oil and water didn't mix.

Too bad an intellectual decision had nothing to do with the vagaries of the heart. For Dominic knew he was falling for the woman who had more courage and tenacity than anyone he'd ever met. A woman who would, in the end, hurt him if he got too close. He still hadn't forgotten how easily Priscilla had left him when things got tough.

In one fell swoop, he'd lost all that had mattered to him—his credibility, his job, his wife and hopes of children in the future. His life had been destroyed by the publicity surrounding his father's trial.

If he were astute, he would give up any fantasies he might have about Asia before they blossomed.

That would be the smart thing to do.

But would he?

MADE UNEASY by the renewal of tension between them—and this time she had no idea of what she'd done—Asia didn't look forward to the hour-long drive. So when they pulled out of the gas station and she spotted the familiar woman hitchhiking up the road, Asia was relieved.

"Let's stop and give her a ride."

Dominic brought the Bronco to a halt a few yards from where the woman with the spiky red hair stood.

Asia poked her head out of the window. "How far are you going?"

"Olympia Grove," the redhead answered, her voice hopeful. "But I'll go as far as you can take me in that direction."

"No problem. We're going all the way."

Asia opened the passenger door. The other woman slid out of her backpack and tossed it into the vehicle before getting in herself. Up close, Asia saw she was attractive without being conventionally pretty. Her features were square, yet softened by large, liquid brown eyes. She wore jeans and an artsy painted T-shirt that showed off her trim, big-boned figure to advantage. And she wore a different and unusual pair of earrings in each of three sets of holes pierced in her lobes.

"I really appreciate this," the woman said, settling back as Dominic pulled the vehicle back onto the road.

"I recognize you," he said, his tone guarded. "You had breakfast at Fanny's this morning."

The woman's brow rose. "Right. So did the two of you. I'm Marijo Lunt."

She held out a hand, which Asia took. The woman's grip was firm and friendly.

"I'm Asia Raferty. And this is Dominic Crawford."

"Nice to meet you. I was hoping I wouldn't have to wait all day before getting a ride. I'm anxious to arrive as early as possible so I have time to get back into the forest. I'm hoping to land a job with Mountain Timber Company."

"It's a small world," Dominic said, glancing back to flash her a suspicious look. "That's exactly where we're headed."

"It is?" Marijo said. "Wow, what a stroke of luck!"

Asia realized the redhead didn't catch the fact that Dominic felt it too neat a coincidence. What was wrong with him? So what if the woman just happened to have the same destination as they did. She hadn't been attacked by a woman. He really was uptight this morning. About to turn the conversation to something more pleasant, she didn't get the opportunity.

"Where did you say you were from?" Dominic demanded of their passenger.

"Originally? Tacoma."

"How about more recently?"

"I move around a lot. Keeps life interesting."

"What made you decide to come this way now?"

"My horoscope told me it was time for a change." A hint of laughter brightened Marijo's voice. "Do you always give strangers the third degree? Or just hitchhikers?"

He didn't answer directly. "A woman hitching alone is unusual."

"Not really," Asia said, feeling she had to defend Marijo since she was the one who suggested they stop for the woman. And Dominic was starting to irritate her.

"Hitching around Europe isn't the same as it is here," he said.

"Who says I haven't hitched in the States?" Asia had, though she hadn't liked it much. Americans had a different view of hitchhiking than Europeans. Not to mention that hitchhiking was illegal in many states.

"So what do you think Mountain Timber will be like?" Asia asked Marijo. "Ever worked for a logging company before?"

"Nope. My first time. But I can make an educated stab at it. My dad was a logger until they shut down Grisdale almost five years back."

"I've heard of Grisdale," Asia said. "One of the old-time lumber camps, right?"

Marijo nodded. "Supposedly the nicest. It was more of a town built for families than a transient camp. But that way of life is gone because it's not economically feasible. Now logging companies have roundup points in various small towns. They bus the loggers out to their sites."

Not ever having seen one of the old logging camps herself, Asia was intrigued. "Was it great growing up in a forest community?"

"I only spent a couple of years at Grisdale, but I remember being happy. Moved out when I was ten. Our parents got divorced, and my sister and I went with Mom. My older brother stayed with Dad, though. Harry works for Weyerhauser now," Marijo said, naming the famous forestry company.

Throughout the ride, the redhead kept them entertained with logging stories—some real, others tall tales. Cheerful and often amusingly outrageous, she lessened the tension in the truck, made Asia forget about the seriousness of her problems for a short while. Dominic even seemed to soften toward her.

When they passed through the busy town of Olympia Grove and drew deep into the forest, following the maze of unpaved logging roads, she was impressed by the stands of hundred-year-old growth, replanted trees that were actually in miniature scale compared to old-growth forests.

Dominic slowed the Bronco and pulled it over to the side of the road to let pass a monster log truck turning wide off a side road. Such working vehicles were common to the Pacific Northwest. Though she knew families counted on the money from logging, Asia had long ago come to hate the flatbed trucks that coffined the bodies of once-living trees.

She was sad every time she spotted one of the many extensive clear-cut patches among the forested mountains, not only on the Olympic Peninsula but throughout the Pacific Northwest. Broken stubs of former cedar and spruce and Douglas fir now poked up from the earth; discarded branches lay rotting on the ground like giant toothpicks. Such destruction left her angry, too, because she always felt as if a piece of her heritage had been bartered away by some already affluent conglomerate.

But she put her environmental concerns behind as they pulled into the Mountain Timber Company commuter camp, which consisted of what looked like several prefabricated buildings—office, cook house and storage. In addition, flatbed trucks were parked to one side of the clearing, tractors and other logging equipment opposite.

They left the truck with several other vehicles a short way from the office. As they approached the building, two loggers wearing hard hats exited, nodding at them in greeting. Dominic held the door open for both women before following them inside.

A giant of a middle-aged man, at least six-two and broad to match, sat at a desk loaded with folders and stacks of loose papers. "Can I help you folks?"

"We're looking for jobs," Dominic said.

"I'm Norman Haskel, camp boss," the ruddy complected man told them. "We're in the midst of expanding our operation, so we have plenty of openings. Take a look at the listings on the bulletin board."

After doing so, they filled out applications and were interviewed by Haskel while other job seekers entered. Asia was relieved when the camp boss hired her and Dominic as well as Marijo. The redhead would waitress at breakfast and lunch; since Asia was familiar with computers, she was set to work in the employment office; and Dominic would drive a tractor, hauling trees from where they were felled to a loading area.

After welcoming each of them on board with a hearty handshake, Haskel asked, "You folks got a place to stay?"

"We don't," Asia said, looking at the three men filling out applications.

The one in the brimmed straw hat looked familiar. She was sure she'd seen him before in Eagle Creek—first at the post office, then at Tully's.

"Neither do I," Marijo added.

"We set up a small trailer park on the north end of Olympia Grove for new workers," Haskel was saying. "Rents are reasonable and you only have to commit yourself for a month at a time. You find something you like better, you can move.''

He handed Dominic a photocopied map with the trailer park's location. Asia followed him and Marijo to the door, her attention fixed on the man who'd finished his application and was now staring at her. His expression was flirtatious, but she had this awful feeling . . .

That Marijo had been heading for the same place they were might have been a coincidence. But what about this man?

So absorbed was she in her speculations that Asia didn't see yet another man coming through the door. She ran smack into him.

''Sorry,'' she said, the word half-swallowed as she looked up into familiar brown eyes.

They belonged to the man wearing a cow skull T-shirt.

Chapter Seven

"Do you think both of those men being here is a co-incidence?" Asia asked when they were finally alone in the small trailer they'd rented. "You did recognize them?"

Dominic nodded. "Could be a coincidence, all of us passing through Eagle Creek on our way here."

And he might even believe it if someone hadn't tried to run down Asia earlier. Added to that incident, the man in the cow skull T-shirt seemed oddly familiar, and Dominic had the nagging feeling he should know the guy.

"I'm beginning to wonder if my confidence wasn't a little overinflated when I set out on this mission."

Sounding and appearing less sure of herself than Dominic had ever thought possible, Asia dropped down to the rugged brown couch that would open to make his bed. As they had been when she'd first intruded in his life, her pale gray blue eyes were shadowed with fear.

"I'm not sure I can get through this."

"I am."

Her brow furrowed. "Why?"

"Because you're the gutsiest lady I've ever met."

"The gutsiest or the pestiest?"

"Maybe both."

Asia laughed at that, the sound a combination of humor and self-consciousness. "At least you're consistently honest."

"It took me a long time to learn it doesn't pay to lie, whether it be about someone else or about yourself." Facing her, he propped himself against the vinyl-topped counter. When she gazed at him steadily, her raised dark eyebrows arched in question, he clarified. "My name. I thought changing it to Crawford was the solution to all my problems. I tried to hide from the truth... but then you know that."

Her pale cheeks flushed and she seemed embarrassed.

"I, uh, may have been a little overzealous when I got on your case about you running away from your past instead of fighting it." She stared at the floor as though fascinated by the multicolored indoor-outdoor carpeting. "I guess I was desperate enough to do or say anything to get your help, even if I had to attack you personally to do it."

"You had your reasons."

"There's no justification to hurt someone, whether it be physically or with words." She swallowed hard and met his gaze directly. "I'm sorry, Dominic. I wasn't playing fair. I even had myself convinced you took the easy way out. I know that isn't true. I can only guess what you went through when you discovered what... or who your father really was. I might have done the same in your situation."

Not really believing she would have, Dominic said, "Apology accepted."

He had an overwhelming and curious need to explain things to Asia. She'd touched a part of him he'd thought dead. She was so damn beautiful it almost hurt to look at her. More important, she had an inner beauty, a richness of spirit that he'd never before recognized in another human being. While he'd condemned his father, she'd forgiven hers. Not that the circumstances were the same. Still, he wasn't certain that he would have been so generous.

Because of his growing feelings for her, he felt it important that she understand the man he had become. He grabbed one of the two kitchen chairs from the small table and twirled it around. Then he sat and leaned forward, chest against the backrest.

"I was a teenager when I realized my father made his living illegally," he began. "Talk about justification—I pretended he didn't actually hurt anyone. I even convinced myself he only profited from people or companies who could afford to lose money."

"You were trying to protect yourself and your relationship with him."

"When I couldn't do that anymore, I told him how much I hated his business, tried to convince him that he could do anything he wanted to make a living. I didn't care if we weren't rich. He laughed at me, said some things that no man should ever say to his son. Unforgivable things." Remembering how hurt and disillusioned he'd been, Dominic shook his head. "That's when I started to hate him."

"And you left home."

"No, not then. I wasn't old enough. I spent a couple more years in that house. Even then my mother was what you would call 'delicate.' I think that was her way of denying what my father was. She could pretend not to know and therefore protect herself while continuing to love him."

"Everyone has a different way of dealing with the pain life deals us," Asia said, sounding as if she knew what she was talking about.

Fueled by the admissions he'd already made, Dominic went on. "That's when Jess and I got really close. She was just a kid, seven years younger than I was. She didn't understand what was tearing me apart, but she always seemed to be there when I needed her. Sometimes she made me laugh. Sometimes she made me furious with her. But she always made me believe she loved me no matter what, that she would always be there for me. I wish to God I could say the same for myself...that I had been there for her two years ago."

"You can't take the burden of the world on your shoulders," Asia said.

"Jess wasn't the world—she was my kid sister." Even as he spoke, he could see her sparkling green eyes lighted with mischief, her lips turned up into a perpetual smile. "I failed her. I didn't make a real effort to find her when she disappeared. I convinced myself that was the way she wanted it, when in reality, she was undoubtedly trying to protect herself because she had no one she could count on. I was too busy worrying about myself."

"But your own life was crumbling around you."

"I lost my job. My wife. What was left of a real mother. I didn't have to lose my sister, as well. You really struck a gold mine when you came after me, Asia. I have so much guilt buried so deeply I don't know if I can ever deal with it all."

"Forgive yourself instead."

Dominic couldn't help the bitter laugh that escaped him. "That's easy to say for someone who has led such an exemplary life."

"I'm no saint."

"What are you guilty of? Pushing to make me face up to my faults?"

Asia rose from the couch and moved to him. "No one is perfect, Dominic. We all make mistakes. All we can do is be the best person we know how."

"Sometimes that isn't enough."

She placed a hand on his shoulder, the contact at once reassuring and intimate. It was the first time she'd voluntarily touched him. Dominic was moved. He covered her long, slender fingers with his own and they communicated silently for a moment. Her skin was soft and sensual against his callused fingertips. He imagined the rest of her was equally seductive.

Then, as if disturbed by the same awareness that passed through Dominic, Asia withdrew her hand and turned her back on him. She picked up her overnight bag, which she'd set down next to the door.

"Since this place won't be jumping until the workers are through for the day, I'm going to unpack and lie down for a while."

"What about getting something to eat?"

"Maybe later."

"Not maybe. Definitely. You need fuel for energy," he reminded her.

Glancing over her shoulder, she shot him a smile. "Later, then. We can go over to MacGregor's," she suggested, naming the multipurpose recreation hall they'd seen as they drove in. "Maybe we'll be lucky enough to run into Peggy Shield there."

Dominic could only hope for such luck. Peggy could have rented a room in town as she had in Eagle Creek. Still, finding the mystery woman couldn't be too hard, not with Asia working in the employment office the next day. Convincing the stranger to reveal the whereabouts of his sister was another problem. But he would manage it, Dominic promised himself. It was imperative that he get Jess back to Seattle where she could intercede with their father before something more could happen to Asia.

The sound of her moving around in the back of the trailer affected him as had happened at Miss Odel's. He wasn't even in the same room with the woman and he couldn't get his mind off her. Maybe if he left the trailer...

He hightailed it out of the claustrophobic old-fashioned box, which was half the size of newer models at best, and he sat on the old wooden stoop.

While Mountain Timber had provided temporary homes for new workers, the accommodations were anything but luxurious. The trailers were well used, most in need of paint or repair. In the case of their unit, the last tenants had left a junk pile outside, including stacks of bound newspapers shoved up against the structure's aluminum side. The sight was depressing, but Dominic figured they wouldn't be around long enough to worry about cleaning up the mess.

The trailer park itself was set in a cul-de-sac cleared from the forest at the edge of town. Although the area had plenty of shade, the landscaping was spotty. Wild grasses grew untended. Rather than a luxurious green, the patch around their trailer was yellowing due to the late-August dry spell. And only individuals interested enough to do the work themselves had small gardens or containers of flowers.

One such woman two lots down was watering the fruits of her labor. Shrubs surrounded the trailer, and a small formal garden of shade-loving flowers provided a bright spot against the gloom. Finished with her task, the woman coiled the hose and left it on the ground below the spigot.

Dominic's gaze roved over the trailer park, coming to rest on the unit Marijo had rented. Leaning against a spruce tree right outside her door, she was talking to a man who was acting pretty friendly for a stranger. He laughed at something she said, then took her arm and led her away. A few yards down the path, he put on his brimmed straw hat.

Dominic bolted off the stoop for a better look. The two seemed to be walking over to MacGregor's. Without a plan in mind, he followed.

The rec hall was busier than he might have expected, due no doubt to the influx of newcomers who had not yet started their jobs. Four men were playing pool, one of them being the guy with the cow skull T-shirt. Another man and a woman were shooting darts. On the sandwich-shop side of the room, Marijo was getting a can of soda and another of beer, while the straw-hatted man picked out some tunes on the nearby jukebox.

"Wanna dance?" he called to her over the country music.

"Nah, I got two left feet," Marijo said. As she turned from the counter, she looked Dominic's way. "Hi, there. All settled in, huh. Where's Asia?"

"Relaxing." He looked over to the guy at the jukebox. "Who's your friend?"

"Name's Eddy Voss," the man said, coming even with Marijo and putting an arm around her shoulders.

The redhead shrugged free and placed a foot of distance between them. She handed him the soda. "We just met, but Eddy's the friendly type."

And Marijo hadn't seemed to mind when she'd gone off with Eddy. The man certainly minded her casual rejection of him now, however. His hazel eyes narrowed unattractively before he laughed and threw himself into a chair at a nearby table. A gold chain glinted from beneath his shirt. That and the expensive watch he wore didn't go with the image of a woodsman.

"C'mon, sit. Let's all get acquainted."

Marijo took the chair opposite Eddy, Dominic one in between. He glanced over at the pool table and realized the guy who looked so familiar was staring at him. Caught, the man looked away and watched the shooter with equal intensity. Dominic had the oddest feeling that all three people were focused on him.

"So, where you from?" Eddy asked, his question boisterous. Removing his hat, he tossed it on the vacant chair.

"Seattle originally," Dominic said. "Now I'm from here."

Eddy raised his can. "Guess we all are. Right, Red?"

"Right," Marijo said, digging a pack of cigarettes from her jeans pocket. "Want one?"

Dominic shook his head, but Eddy loudly declared, "Weeds never touch my lips." He flexed his muscles, making it apparent he was a bodybuilder. His mobile face held more than a hint of pride when he said, "The body is a temple. And this is a pretty good one, ain't it, sweetheart?"

"As good as they come," Marijo agreed, tapping out a cigarette for herself. "Personally, I like my vices too much to worry about temples and such."

After she lighted up, she threw the matches on the table, giving Dominic a start when he saw Tully's Tap and Grill emblazoned across the packaging. So Marijo had been in the bar, too. The night before? With Eddy, this man who was supposedly a stranger?

"I've spent most of my life working on this one," Eddy went on, flexing some more. "I've won a few contests in my time. What about you, Dominic? Do any lifting?"

"Yeah, sixty-pound crates," he answered, thinking about the job he'd just lost.

Noticing the guy with the cow skull T-shirt was bellying up to the refreshment counter, Dominic rose.

"I'm thirsty. Think I'll get myself a beer." Once at the counter, he lost no time in introducing himself. "Name's Dominic Crawford."

He held out his hand until the other man was obligated to take it.

"George Yerkes."

"We've met before, haven't we?"

"Don't think so."

But Yerkes quickly looked away. So that Dominic couldn't read the lie in his face?

"So what did Haskel hire you to do?"

"Logger. What else?" Yerkes answered tersely. To the young woman behind the counter, he said, "Another Old Style."

"Make that two."

Yerkes was a leanly muscled man a little under six feet and of average looks. Nothing distinguished about him other than the T-shirt. Medium brown hair and eyes. Mid-thirties, Dominic guessed. A man who could easily blend in to a crowd. Though Yerkes was ignoring him, Dominic wasn't going to let the guy off so easily. He propped an elbow on the counter, moved into the other man's line of vision and stared intently.

"I'd swear I've seen you before. Where did you say you were from?"

"I didn't."

The young woman came back with the two beers. Taking his, Yerkes threw his money on the counter and stalked off without saying another word.

"Not too friendly, is he?" the girl commented in a soft voice. "By the way, I'm Sandy."

Dominic took the cue from her. She obviously wanted to talk. "Some people are a little standoffish, Sandy. You probably meet all kinds working here."

"All that live in this trailer court, anyhow."

Dominic decided to take the chance of being direct without telling any tall tales. "Then you know Peggy Shield."

The young woman's brow wrinkled. "Peggy... I don't think so. No," she said more certainly. "How long ago did she live here?"

"I just assumed she lived here now. She left Eagle Creek last week to work for Mountain Timber."

"Well, she might have taken a room in town. And there's a couple of folks with some acreage along the main road who take boarders to supplement their incomes, too."

So unless they found her at Mountain Timber, they had their work cut out for them.

"I'm sure we'll catch up with her tomorrow when we report for work." Or so he hoped. About to head back to his table, Dominic took yet another chance. "What about her friend?" he asked with an amiable smile. "Now what was her name?" He pretended to think for a moment. "I believe it was Jessica. Medium height. On the thin side, but a real looker. Chestnut hair, big green eyes..."

He didn't continue because the woman was already shaking her head. "Haven't seen anyone who fits that description, either."

"Thanks anyway, Sandy."

Dominic left the counter in time to catch Yerkes turning his back. For all his seeming indifference, the guy *had* been watching him. As was Eddy Voss, though the muscle-bound man made no bones about it. His hazel eyes glittered as though in some unspoken challenge. When Marijo glanced in Dominic's direction, he could swear she was nervous. She covered fast and gave him a bright smile.

"So what are your plans for the rest of the day?" she asked.

"I think I'm going to take this back to the trailer." Dominic indicated his beer. "See you guys later."

"Later, pal," Eddy agreed, amusement ripe in his voice.

The hair rose on the back of Dominic's neck as he left the place, but he didn't bother turning around to see how many of the three were watching him with undivided interest. He wanted to get back to Asia, to assure himself that she was all right. Something had gone wrong directly under their noses. They'd been fools to think no one knew where they were...that no one would find them.

Asia wasn't safe, not by a long shot.

The thought ate at Dominic's gut like the cancer that was wasting his father. He couldn't tolerate the idea that his own father might be responsible for killing the woman who'd pestered her way into his heart. For Dominic knew that he was a fool. He wasn't just falling for the blonde, he was already down for the count. He'd hardly touched Asia, had never even kissed her, and yet he was afraid he might actually be in love.

What an impossible situation. Nothing could ever come of his feelings. He was a Crawley. But if he couldn't have her love, at least he could protect her. So far, he hadn't done a very good job of it.

Not when someone in Eagle Creek had tried to run her down and he hadn't even been there to get her out of harm's way.

Wondering if he could talk her into driving the Bronco back to Seattle while he alone looked for Peggy and then Jessica, Dominic knew it would be an exercise in futility. Asia would never agree. So how was he going to protect her when he was certain that one of the three strangers who'd come here through that town was the deadly driver?

But which one?

And until he figured it out, how was he going to keep her safe?

A TROUBLED SYDNEY RAFERTY looked out over Seattle from the terrace of the family home on Queen Anne's Hill as dusk settled over the city.

Dusk, a place halfway between darkness and light, ignorance and knowledge. Once again she knew too much for her own peace of mind…and yet not enough to be of help to her sister. If only her premonitions and visions were more concrete. If only she could discuss them with her father.

That, of course, was impossible. Judge Jasper Rafferty was ever the skeptic. He would never change.

Needing to talk to someone, she went inside to the nearest telephone and dialed Dakota's number. To her relief, he rather than his machine answered.

"It's me," she said, voice trembling.

"Syd, what's wrong?"

"I don't know exactly, but Asia's in trouble."

"You mean more than we already know about?"

"Much more."

Her ears rang with Dakota's curses before he asked, "What did you see?"

A little more than a month ago he might have tried to tease her out of her mood. That he didn't now indicated how seriously he took her.

"A dark space," she finally said. "I sensed rather than saw."

"Sensed what?"

"Her terrible fear. Dakota, I can't stand this…this not knowing."

"Syd, hold on." Her brother sounded relieved. "Maybe you were reliving what happened to you—"

"No! This was different." The same, but different. Threat everywhere. A sense of urgency once removed. "We have to warn Asia that she's still in danger."

"I wish to God we could, but we don't exactly know where she is. And if we don't know," he added reasonably, "then neither does anyone else."

But Sydney could tell Dakota didn't believe that any more than she did. Evil had a way of seeking out and finding the innocent victim, as they both had experienced so very recently.

"What are we going to do?" she asked.

"Until we hear from her, all we can do is pray we can find some way of forcing Crawley's hand, some way to make him call off his goons."

"How does one get that kind of leverage on a man who seems to care about nothing or no one but his own thirst for vengeance?"

ASIA LAY IN THE DARK seeking sleep. Despite her body's exhaustion, her mind wouldn't cooperate and shut down. Dominic had behaved so oddly toward her that evening. Protective yet distant. Definitely aggravating.

Having already checked out MacGregor's, he'd taken her into town for dinner. Any camaraderie they'd felt while plotting their strategy for the next day had ended when he'd strongly suggested she return to Seattle and safety while he did the investigating.

They'd driven back to the trailer park in stony silence.

Silence.

Rearranging herself in bed, she tried to concentrate on the all-enveloping quiet of the surrounding woods, tried to lose herself in the occasional hushed murmur of tree branches against the wind. She was starting to drift...

A set of impatient creaks coming from the other room startled her eyes open.

Asia turned over and plumped up her pillows yet again. She wondered if Dominic was having an equally difficult time sleeping because of the sofa bed...or because of her.

They'd retired without speaking.

She'd felt so close to him that morning, and she'd sworn he'd felt the same. What had happened to put this chasm between them? She imagined the evening ending in a very different way. With her in his arms. With him in her bed.

Longing competed with loathing, the memory haunting her of how the stranger's hands had probed and hurt her. Tears stung the back of her eyelids and she swallowed hard. Would she ever get over this fear a criminal had forced upon her? Couldn't she even indulge in some innocent daydreaming about an attractive man.

The snap of a twig almost directly outside her window changed the direction of her thoughts and skittered her pulse. Throbbing with sudden anxiety, she listened intently and heard a soft crunch. A footfall? Who would be walking through the park in the middle of the night? Try as she might, she heard nothing more and decided some small nocturnal animal must be rooting around, searching for food. A raccoon, perhaps. They were on the edge of the forest, after all.

Besides, she wasn't alone. Dominic was stretched out in the other room, for the moment as awake as she. No one could get to her without getting past him.

That settled, she closed her eyes and tried a meditation technique Sydney had taught her. She concentrated on peaceful images and soothing sounds. Ocean waves curled and spit white foam. The rush of water surged onto a fine-grained sand beach. A refreshing breeze countered the warmth of the sun. Within minutes her pulse stabilized, her breathing relaxed.

That was it, she thought, as lethargy crept through her limbs. Now take a nice deep breath.

In . . . out. Deeper. In . . .

This intake of air scratched at her lungs, made her release it with a sharp cough. Sitting up, she sniffed and found the atmosphere laden with the thick, acrid smell of fire.

Frowning, she checked the bedside clock whose glow-in-the-dark numbers assured her the hour was well past midnight. They needed to awaken by six. Why would someone start a campfire so late? Asia wondered. Because she was becoming uncomfortable, she threw off the bedcovers.

Suddenly realizing what she'd just done—how unusually warm the room was becoming—Asia jumped out of bed.

"Dominic!" She ran to the high window, and standing on her tiptoes, looked out. Her gaze met no more than an ominous glow, but the wall was hot to the touch. "My God. A fire. We're on fire!"

The words were barely out of her mouth before Dominic rushed into the room and trapped her wrist in his large callused hand. "C'mon, we've got to get out of here."

"But I'm not dressed."

He paused only to grab the bedcovers. Thinking he meant to wrap the material around them, Asia became confused when he headed into the bathroom.

"What are you doing?" she demanded.

"Trying to save our lives."

Dominic turned on the shower and pulled her into the stall with him. Asia shrieked as the icy pellets hit her, but he didn't let go until they and the covers were soaked. She sensed his anger—not with her, but with their predicament—and his fear. She was attuned to his emotions, couldn't miss the flare of his deeper, personal response to her as opposed to the dangerous situation when his eyes flicked over the front of her nightshirt where her nipples had hardened in reaction to the cold.

Dominic wanted her. In the midst of grave danger, the crazy man wanted her!

And Asia was amazed to feel herself respond as she glimpsed his skimpy white briefs, which molded him as intimately. Instinctively her body reacted with equal vigor even while Dominic ended the fleeting and silent acknowledgment of their mutual attraction. He guided her back out of the cubicle and toward the front door.

"Stand back," he ordered, placing himself between her and immediate danger.

Holding the wet blanket in front of him like a shield, he cracked open the door. Fire danced over the grounds, greedily consuming the dried grasses. Even closer, the stoop blazed brightly.

Asia tasted bile that rose in her throat. "We're trapped. We can't get out through those flames."

"We have to. Unless you want to be roast meat for scavengers."

With that, Dominic threw the blanket over the stoop and burning ground, giving them a clear if smoldering path. Tenting them with the sheet, he shoved her out the door first, one hand staying at her waist as he followed. Wet heat seared the bottom of her bare feet,

Asia glanced over her shoulder. The stack of newspapers and other junk had made a perfect bonfire at one end of the trailer. The dried grass had spread the flames around the base. When they were clear of the lot, Dominic let go of her and shoved the wet sheet into her hands.

"Stay put." He ran off, yelling, "Fire!"

Asia joined the alert. "Fire! Wake up, everyone! Fire!"

Hoping she could stop the conflagration from spreading, she began hitting at the edges of the burning ground cover with the wet sheet. Tiny flames flickered and died but continued to smoke. From the corner of her eye she saw Dominic. He was running back toward her, something in one hand. He reached forward with the other and a spray of water whooshed out the nozzle of a garden hose.

"Hey, what's going on out here?" a sleepy if aggravated voice asked.

Dominic aimed the stream of water at the junk pile.

People were responding, coming out of their trailers, reacting fast. Another hose appeared. Buckets of water. Within minutes the fire was out. And, as far as Asia could tell in the dim glow provided by a nearby jury-rigged streetlight, the damage to the structure itself was minimal. Its bottom blackened, the trailer looked like a giant aluminum cooking pot directly off the stove.

"What happened?" asked a woman who wrapped a bathrobe tightly around her portly body.

"Don't know," the young man with the second hose answered. He was still spraying the area with water, as was Dominic. "Some kind of spontaneous combustion."

"More 'n likely, someone was stupid enough to toss a cigarette before making sure it was out." This from an old guy wearing long underwear and holding a bucket. "You folks is lucky you weren't asleep. Coulda been burned to a crisp."

Asia shuddered, a combination of reaction and chill. The nightshirt still clung to her and sent rivulets of cold water down her bare legs.

"Thank you all for reacting so fast," Dominic said. He was flooding the junk pile with more water. "Go on back to bed. We'll be all right."

Arms wrapped around her chest, Asia watched the small crowd disperse. People were still speculating on how the fire had started. She wondered if the person responsible was there watching. Laughing inside. For she was certain this had been no accident.

Thinking she caught a glimpse of the man she now knew to be George Yerkes, Asia squinted hard. The light was so dim she couldn't be certain. And then the man disappeared into the dark. She turned to Dominic.

Finally appearing to be satisfied that everything was saturated so that the fire couldn't rekindle itself, he turned off the water and returned the hose to the nearby lot. Meanwhile Asia picked up what was left of her blanket and stared at the charred wet material.

"He wants me dead."

Stunned by the knowledge that King Crawley's henchman had indeed found her—and that the racketeer was obviously trying to punish her for having escaped the rape—she couldn't move. Her stomach clenched, and a fist closed around her heart. She'd known she was in danger. Why did this surprise her?

"Maybe that was the point all along," she whispered numbly, wondering how one human being could be so callous. "Maybe he always meant for me to die after making me suffer."

A wet arm slipped around her back. "Leave it," Dominic said.

Unsure as to whether he meant the blanket or the black thoughts, Asia undid her fist and let the water-weighted material snap to the ground.

"Let's go inside, Asia."

Trying not to shake, she moved automatically to Dominic's instructions. He flipped on a light in the living room and closed the door. She didn't fight him when he gathered her in his arms, rubbing her back, murmuring her name. Nor did she respond. She stood there, wooden, trying to make her mind a blank.

"I'm so sorry," he whispered. "I wish I could have spared you this. I meant to keep you safe. God, Asia, if anything had happened to you . . ."

A large callused hand cradled her face, tilted it up so that her gaze met Dominic's. She was surprised by the expression she saw in his eyes. She'd expected anger and regret, but not this tenderness.

Where did all this soft emotion come from?

His eyes drew closer. And his mouth. His lips brushed hers once . . . then again.

When she didn't resist, they made contact. Warmth spread through her mouth at the touch of his tongue on hers. He played a gentle game that countered the taut intensity she felt grip his body. She responded slowly. Tentatively. Afraid. Yet needing the reassurance that someone cared what happened to her. The reassurance that she was still alive.

Her heart beat sharply in her throat, a combination of excitement and something darker.

Dominic deepened the kiss only for a moment. When she might have protested, he lifted his head and swept her back into the bathroom and shower, this time to be pelted by water that was warm and soothing. Only when he lifted the hem of her nightshirt did she snap out of her trancelike state.

"No!"

Wide-eyed, she grabbed his wrist. Hard. Her heart accelerated as they stood locked in a silent struggle of wills. Fear whipped through her. He was strong. He could force her. No matter that she'd been attracted to him barely a half hour before.

He was a man, no different than any other.

"You're filthy and cold," Dominic said reasonably. "You need to get cleaned up and warm. I'm not going to hurt you, Asia. I promise."

"No," she said more softly, though she didn't release her grip on his wrist.

His face a purposeful blank, Dominic backed off and pulled his arm free. "Then I'll get one of my shirts and hang it on the door for you."

Asia almost stopped him. Almost called him back to explain. To apologize for having hurt him.

Almost.

She couldn't make herself utter the words that would put voice to her confusion. She'd allowed Dominic to soothe her, to kiss her, had even responded for a moment. She didn't want to be detached. Or fearful.

She wanted...what, to turn back time? To go back to being an innocent who'd trusted men? Erasing what his father's goon had tried to do to her was never going to happen.

And if she were able to change history, that would mean she wouldn't know Dominic, a little voice inside her whispered as she stripped off the nightshirt and let it drop to the floor of the shower stall.

Which would be worse—to be without Dominic or to take a chance that she might not survive the knowing?

Asia was terrified of the answer.

AFTER LEAVING one of his clean shirts on the bathroom doorknob as he'd promised, Dominic threw on his jeans and T-shirt and climbed into his shoes, while trying to block out the sound of running water and the accompanying fantasies. Then he grabbed a flashlight and escaped both the trailer and his disturbing proximity to Asia.

He had to get away from her for a short while. Away from the emotions that were tearing up his gut. Feelings Asia didn't share.

Not that he'd expected her to.

Yet when she'd responded to his kiss he'd thought... hell, he'd been a fool to think anything of the embrace. She'd wanted comforting and he'd been at hand. Rafertys and Crawleys didn't mix.

When would the simple concept penetrate his thick skull?

He circled the trailer, which looked every bit the center of a disaster zone. The ground was charred and wet, the air sharp and humid. Being cooked inside the thing would have been a horrifying death. And the situation might have gone that way if they hadn't both lain awake long after exhaustion should have claimed them.

Luck.

Flicking on the flashlight, Dominic stared at the former junk pile turned ash, and realized how lucky they both were to have escaped with their lives. Now if only he could be lucky enough to discover the identity of the person who had tried to torch them.

Then what? Go to the local authorities, introduce himself and ask them to keep the bastard locked up until they had their problem solved?

The soggy ground squished under his feet as Dominic came full circle. He was certain the fire had been started using the bundled newspapers, so he stopped at that spot and took several steps back. Then he flicked the beam around. Of course he saw nothing revealing in the wet, black mess. If he were to find something—a clear footprint, even—it would undoubtedly be outside the burned area.

Honest with himself, Dominic admitted recognizing a footprint would be an impossible task. The people who'd come to their rescue had trampled the ground pretty thoroughly. There would be dozens, maybe hundreds, of footprints. So why bother with a useless search?

Driven to defy the odds, he kept looking, carefully zigzagging back and forth, inching away from the trailer a bit at a time. A moment later he was rewarded when the beam of his flashlight caught a bright spot against the dark earth. Instinct curled his gut with excitement, and he stooped for a closer look.

The object slid from the muck with a sucking sound; he flicked away a blob of mud. Letting loose a whistle, he stared at the familiar red lettering.

Tully's Tap and Grill.

Chapter Eight

"Hey, I could drive this thing smoother with one hand tied behind my back!" Eddy Voss yelled after the truck hit a pothole that set Asia's teeth on edge.

"Yeah, and you could walk the rest of the way, too," the driver growled.

Eddy merely laughed in response and the men around him snickered.

Crummies—company-owned crew trucks with padded bench seats—were hauling the workers to the logging site from various towns as far away as Aberdeen. Asia felt a sense of unreality as theirs jounced along the gravel access road that tunneled them deep into the forest. She could hardly believe she and Dominic were going through with the plan after almost having been barbecued the night before.

Not that they'd actually discussed the advisability of carrying on as if nothing had happened.

Next to her, Dominic sat in silence, withdrawn as he'd been all morning. They'd hardly spoken to each other since rising. Knowing she'd hurt him when she'd panicked in the shower, Asia felt a stab of guilt every time she glanced at his hard expression. He, no doubt, assumed she'd rejected him because of who he was—

rather who his father was—when nothing could be farther from the truth.

Fear had made her stop him. Fear instigated by a man whose face she wouldn't recognize if she saw it.

Experienced in hiding information he didn't want other people to know, Dominic was doing an especially fine job of it with her. She hadn't a clue as to how he felt about her now, after having had time to stew about what had gone on between them in the shower. Not that he'd ever said in the first place. The subject hadn't come up.

And if he had any opinion on the identity of the arsonist, he wasn't sharing that with her, either.

To get her mind off Dominic, Asia focused on one of the suspects.

Eddy Voss sat three seats ahead. Every so often, the man glanced back at her, all smiles and mocking self-confidence. Once, he'd even had the audacity to wink. Was he really the harmless braggart and flirt he seemed—or was this a cover for a darker nature? Somehow, she didn't think he was exactly what he appeared to be.

On the other side of the aisle, one seat back, George Yerkes stared studiously out the window. Avoiding them for a reason, perhaps—as he had the night before? The man was quiet, a loner, but Asia sensed he could take care of himself as well as any unwanted "problems."

Only one suspect was missing—if Marijo could be considered such. Asia didn't really think so. After all, she'd been attacked by a man intent on raping her, not by a woman. As part of the cook-house staff and therefore one of the people responsible for getting breakfast together for the loggers, Marijo had departed the trailer park on an earlier pickup.

Taking a sharp turn, the crummy chugged into the Mountain Timber lot. The driver parked it alongside several other similar vehicles and behind a couple of old yellow school buses. Even before he switched off the engine, the workers began filing out of the truck and heading for the cook house.

Asia started to follow until she glanced at Dominic. He cocked his head and hung back, indicating he wanted to tell her something. Complying, she realized he was being extra careful not to touch her as he normally might.

They kept walking at a moderate pace, and the others raced ahead of them. When Dominic spoke, it was in a tone meant only for her ears.

"Whatever you do today, make sure you stay around other people."

Disappointed that he had nothing more personal to say, that he felt it necessary to warn her instead, she felt her ire rise. Why did he dance around what was really bothering him? Couldn't he have a moment's honesty? She didn't bother to cover her annoyance.

"I'm going to be working in an office with plenty of other people coming and going, for heaven's sake!"

"Be careful anyway," he growled. "And don't let anyone catch you snooping. I'll try asking around about Peggy if I'm given the chance."

Asia matched his hostile expression with one of her own.

"I'm not the only one who'd better be careful. Whoever torched the newspaper pile intended to fry us both. You'll be in a much more vulnerable position than I will." The very thought that he would be an easy target worried her. "If I were you," she said stiffly, "I'd watch my back."

She wished she could continue the conversation, turn the topic to the personal, expose the real reason for this manufactured irritation between them. She didn't have the chance. They'd reached the cook house and other sets of ears. Norman Haskel was standing outside the door, greeting the new arrivals. Smiling broadly, he slapped one guy on the back, then turned to Dominic and Asia, who would be the last ones to go inside.

"The crummies leave for the site in less than fifteen minutes, so chow down while you can," he announced. "I don't want any workers complaining about being hungry. Canteen trucks will bring lunch out to the site with sandwiches and stuff a little before noon."

Sweeping ahead of Dominic, Asia gave the camp boss a blinding smile and was rewarded by a like response.

Once inside the dining room, which was already filled to capacity, she looked over the serving staff and cooks and wondered if one of the women could be Peggy. They couldn't very well have asked Miss Odel or Marcie what the mystery woman looked like when Asia was supposedly her sister.

They sat to a breakfast served family-style, with platters of griddle cakes, muffins, bacon, hashed brown potatoes and scrambled eggs being passed around. To Asia's surprise, some of the women sharing the meal seemed to be dressed for the field rather than the office. Women loggers. Things really had changed in the timber industry.

Some things, she amended. At the next table, Eddy was acting the consummate chauvinist by grabbing hold of Marijo's wrist. He was saying something to her, but though Asia was only a few yards away, she couldn't hear above the noisy crowd. Then Marijo wrenched her wrist free and stalked away, while Eddy snickered and returned to his breakfast.

"Did you see that?" Dominic asked in a low voice.

"Eddy Voss is full of himself, all right."

"I've been wondering . . . the two of them seem to know each other."

"Or maybe Eddy just wants to get to know Marijo better," Asia countered, remembering his flirtatious behavior with her. "Some men don't know when to let it alone."

"Maybe," Dominic said, not sounding at all convinced.

Asia took her cue from Dominic, who concentrated on downing his breakfast. But while the odors were tempting, the food seemed flavorless. She was too nervous to enjoy it. And too aware of Dominic's knee as it grazed hers with seeming regularity.

To distract herself, she looked around the large room, past Eddy to the table beyond, where George Yerkes was sitting. Obviously ready to leave, workers were already rising. The lean man followed suit and went with the small crowd. She would have sworn he avoided looking her way. This time she was doing the staring.

And Eddy Voss caught her at it. She realized his expression was speculative when he glanced after Yerkes as the man passed them.

Just then, Norman Haskel entered the dining room through the crowd of men leaving. "Time's up!" he yelled. "New people, report to crew foreman Sam Jepsen before boarding. Before we take you out to the site, he'll assign hard hats to anyone who doesn't have his own. The cost will be deducted from your first paycheck."

Dominic pushed back his chair. "That's me."

Eddy was on his way out before Asia rose. The brash man winked at her as he strode past. A flare of anger made her cheeks burn.

Then a lump gathered in her throat as she and Dominic left the cook house, the two suspect men rapidly outdistancing them as they strode toward the waiting foreman. Unable to help herself, Asia put out a staying hand and wrapped her fingers around Dominic's forearm. She couldn't let him go off like this, without his knowing she cared what happened to him. His safety was too important for her to play any games with him, even verbal ones.

He stopped and looked at her questioningly, his green eyes soft rather than mocking—or what would have been even worse, expressionless.

"Be careful, Dom, please," she said softly.

"Don't worry, I can take care of myself."

Before he could issue another warning in return, she said, "Me, too."

A momentary pause made her think he wanted to say something more, especially when he put a thumb to her cheek and slid the callused tip across her skin. Heat slid through her, opposing the cool morning air. She sensed he wanted to take her in his arms, perhaps even kiss her goodbye. She raised her hand to touch his fingers . . .

"Crawford, you want this job or not?"

"Coming!" Dominic dropped his hand and backed off. "Good luck," he whispered.

Then he tore his gaze from hers and loped toward the crummies, most of which were already headed out of the lot. A knot of fear forming in her stomach, Asia stood and watched while he checked in with the foreman. She hoped he wasn't walking willingly into an even more dangerous situation than they'd been involved in the night before.

If only there was another way.

Dominic found a hard hat, signed for it and covered his chestnut hair, putting the finishing touch on his logger's uniform. His red-and-black plaid shirt strained across his back as he climbed in the truck without looking her way.

Her heart doing a queer little dance in her chest, Asia headed for the office building where other employees entered through various doors. Haskel waited outside the employment office for her.

"All set for a busy day?" he asked, leading the way inside and to the messy desk. "You'll have to haul...uh, work hard to get caught up. No sooner do I train a new girl than she up and quits on me." He indicated the computer. "I have a stack of data that needs entering. I hope you're as quick with one of these things as you said you were."

"I am. Show me what to do."

Asia was overjoyed once she realized the data to be entered were employee evaluations by supervisors. That meant she would have easy access to all employee records. First chance she got she would bring up Peggy Shield's file.

In the process of showing her how the program worked, Haskel was interrupted twice by people seeking work. The camp boss left only once for a quick trip to the men's room, but in the meantime, one of the secretaries from another office came in to look for some forms. And then Haskel returned. Asia was beginning to wonder if she would ever have the opportunity to get at those records. Between job seekers and the telephone, the place remained busy until half past ten.

Finally the office quieted some.

"Think you can handle things here for a while if I go to the site?" Haskel asked.

"Sure," Asia agreed more casually than she felt. This was the opportunity she'd been waiting for. "What if more people come in looking for jobs?"

"Give them applications and tell them to come back with everything filled in. Space appointments out, starting at two this afternoon. That should give me enough time to check things over."

"If someone calls for you, what should I tell them?"

"That I'm out in the field." The camp boss put on his hard hat. "Take messages. If you run into a tight spot, go into the office next door and ask Carol for help."

Haskel was barely out the door when Asia closed down the file she was working on and entered data to bring up Peggy Shield's. She held her breath while the computer searched. It seemed to take forever. Then the screen filled with the information she was seeking.

"She does work here!" Asia said, congratulating herself until she found the termination notice. "I don't believe this!"

Peggy Shield had been employed by Mountain Timber in this very same job for barely a week—the girl who'd left as soon as Haskel trained her. Her last day of work had been the day Asia and Dominic arrived in Eagle Creek. Why had she quit? Coincidence? Or had someone from Eagle Creek warned the woman her "sister and brother-in-law" were looking for her? That would have put her on her guard.

Could Peggy have figured out someone was looking for Jessica and was loyal enough to quit a job to protect her friend?

Asia tried to take solace in the fact that Peggy was only two days ahead of them rather than an entire week. For some reason, she didn't feel the margin between them narrowing.

Determined to get everything possible out of her find, she read over the entire file carefully, starting with the limited physical description that was part of every application. Peggy was five-five, one hundred and fifteen pounds, light brown hair, hazel eyes, glasses, twenty-three years old. The required employment references only went back two jobs. Peggy had worked for two other logging operations in the past year and a half. Nothing before that. No way to figure out where she was from. Not that she had necessarily gone home.

Frustrated, Asia closed down the file as the telephone began ringing. She answered and took a message, then gave out an application when a young woman arrived looking for work.

Now what? With Peggy gone, Asia wondered if working at Mountain Timber was necessary. What were the chances that Peggy had told anyone where she was off to? Staring at the computer screen, which held no answers for her, Asia decided to take advantage of the opportunity to see what else she could find.

On a whim, she entered Jessica Crawley's name. The computer searched... and brought up the file! Asia almost fell off her chair. She scanned the screen quickly. Another termination notice dated several weeks before. Jessica had worked in the cook house for almost six months! Her references were the same as Peggy's—the two women had worked together at other logging operations in the past! No doubt, that's how they had met.

On a roll, Asia went on to Marijo, not really expecting to find anything startling. As far as Asia could tell, everything was in order. Her job references were restaurants in small peninsula towns. She jotted down their names.

After bringing up the file for Yerkes, Asia quickly scanned his job references. Both were with logging companies in Oregon. She added them to her list.

The phone rang again, distracting her just as she brought up Eddy Voss's file. She took a message while she scanned his background. The year before he'd worked at a sawmill job in Tacoma and more recently a logging operation in Shelton, a nearby town to the east.

She was just hanging up the phone when a footfall behind her made her jump.

"Hey, beautiful. All alone?"

Whipping around in her chair, Asia was horrified to see Eddy Voss standing there as if he owned the place. Her pulse pounded as he stepped closer to the desk, stopping a mere yard away from her—and the computer!

"Only for the moment," Asia bluffed.

She wasn't certain Eddy had been able to see the computer screen before she'd become aware of his presence. Now he had a clear shot at it. Carefully checking out his expression, she didn't think he knew what she was up to. If she closed the file under his nose, she would only bring his attention to the fact that she was trying to hide something. Instead she stood to block his view with her body.

"If you're looking for Mr. Haskel—"

"He's at the logging site. I know."

Asia picked up a folder and paged through it without really seeing the contents. "Then is there something I can help you with?"

"I thought I could do something for you . . . if you give me the chance."

"What's that?"

"Why don't I tell you later? Tonight."

"Great." Setting down the folder, she gave him a fake smile. "I'm certain Dominic will be interested in what you have to say, as well."

His normally mobile face set in a disbelieving grimace, Eddy said, "C'mon, babe, you and me. You know that's what I'm talking about. We could make the earth move."

"I don't think so. Besides, I thought your taste ran to redheads."

"You mean Marijo? Jealous, huh?"

"Not jealous. Curious."

Eddy relaxed. "Don't worry about Marijo. She's a cute kid, but you're more my type. Believe me, blondie, I can promise you a ride like you've never had before." When she merely arched her brows in response, he laughed. "You think about it and let me know you're interested. I gotta get going before Haskel wonders what's taking me so long. I'm picking up some equipment,'' he explained.

Legs shaky, Asia sat back in her chair only after he left the office. And then she had to take care of two more applicants and another telephone call before she was able to get back to the computer.

Eddy's Shelton work reference especially bothered her. That town was to the east of the logging area while Eagle Creek was west. Why would he have gone out of his way to get here when he supposedly had been at the other job the week before? She asked directory assistance for the telephone number of Skinner Forest Products, whose personnel office she then called. She pretended to be checking on his references for Mountain Timber.

What she learned was not unexpected: no record of Eddy Voss having worked at Skinner. The story was the same with the sawmill.

No doubt Eddy didn't know the first thing about logging!

Norman Haskel had been so harried he hadn't checked out any of the applicants the day before. Asia knew why she and Dominic had lied.

What was Eddy's reason?

On a roll, she quickly got the numbers of the Oregon companies listed by Yerkes. The more recent reference told her George Yerkes had never been employed by the company. The other was a different story, however. Yerkes had worked as a tree faller, but that had been many years before.

Asia supposed the man might have been out of work all that time and had fudged to get this job.

Anxious to tell Dominic what she'd learned, she decided to go to the logging site to find him. There was no use in waiting until the end of the day to quit. They might as well leave immediately and get back on Peggy's trail. If one of the men followed, they would know who to blame for the fire and the aborted hit and run.

From her desk, the window gave her a clear view of the cook house. The staff was in the process of loading the two canteen trucks. She was thinking she could hitch a ride on one of them when she spotted Marijo setting a basket of fruit on a tailgate.

Seeing her reminded Asia that she hadn't checked on the redhead, hadn't thought it necessary because Marijo was a woman. About to go find Carol to have someone take over the employment office, she hesitated and stared at the slip of paper with the names of the companies that incriminated the two men as being liars if not worse. She might as well finish the job and check out Marijo so she could discount the woman as a suspect.

Picking up the receiver, she dialed directory assistance once more. A few minutes later, her curiosity was satisfied—but her sense of victory went begging.

Neither of the two restaurant owners had ever heard of a Marijo Lunt.

HAVING BEEN PUT THROUGH his paces on the tractor by Sam Jepsen, Dominic was cleared to take a turn at skidding a felled tree to the landing where it would be loaded onto a flatbed truck. Luckily for him he'd had plenty of practice running a tractor the spring before when he'd worked for a farmer planting crops. Now all he had to do was keep his mind on his work, a difficult task at best.

Thoughts of Asia and of their search kept running through his head. The longer it took them to find Peggy, the more danger Asia would be in. He'd figured working for the timber company would give them the best opportunity to find his sister's friend, but so far, no luck. He'd casually mentioned her name to a few of the women loggers, but none had ever heard of a Peggy Shield.

As other workers helped him undo the cables from the log, he hoped Asia was faring better.

Done with his first run, Dominic aimed the tractor back along the crude road that would take him into the thick of the forest and away from the diesel-powered crane that was now loading a log onto a flatbed. Even at this distance he heard the distinctive *thwunk* of a hundred-and-some-foot tree hitting underbrush. He thought it a shame that old growth was so readily destroyed. A chain saw took approximately ninety seconds to slice through a tree that had been alive for a century or more.

At least Mountain Timber was using selective-cutting rather than clear-cutting methods. Only trees marked with a spray gun would be felled—about a fifth of the growth—before the crew would move on to another section of the forest.

As he drew closer to the area being worked, the foreman waved him to the right.

After turning the tractor, he checked the teams of men nearby but didn't spot Eddy. He hadn't seen Eddy since Haskel sent him back to camp for replacement equipment after one of the crosscut saws broke down and a couple of cables snapped. Dominic couldn't help worrying, though he kept telling himself Asia would be all right. People wandered in and out of the employment office all day, and there were other workers next door. If Eddy were the guilty one, surely he wouldn't be stupid enough to try anything in broad daylight.

Dominic kept going until he spotted Yerkes waving him over. He and his partner had felled a tree and were now sawing off limbs. As if he knew exactly what he was doing, Yerkes worked with the same efficiency as the man in the red flannel shirt.

Dominic stopped the tractor nearby, then maneuvered it into position so the winch was at the end of the trunk. He jumped down from the cab and helped the two men secure the log with cables.

The sun was high, the late morning unusually hot. Sweat trickled down Dominic's back. Red-faced under his hard hat, Yerkes had opened his long-sleeved shirt. The plaid material was still held in place by suspenders and the rough hide pad on his left shoulder meant to cradle and protect him from the weight and heat of the twenty-pound saw he carried. Log secured, Yerkes stepped back and removed his thick leather gloves.

"Gets any hotter, we'll roast in our own juices."

Yerkes pulled out the bottom of his T-shirt and used it to wipe his face dry. Dominic got a good look at the guy's chest, decorated with tattoos, one of which disturbed him. He was sure he'd seen the design before. On Yerkes? From the first time he'd spotted the lean man, Dominic had thought Yerkes looked familiar. That he still couldn't place the guy didn't mean a damn thing.

Not after having gotten a glimpse of the tattooed snake wrapped around the shaft of a knife.

"So how long have you and Dominic been together?" Marijo asked as the canteen truck bounced along the access road on the way to the logging site.

"For a while," Asia evaded, for the first time uncomfortable with the other woman.

No matter that instinct told her Marijo was innocent, she'd been proven as much a liar as Eddy Voss or George Yerkes. Asia had tried to avoid the other woman, but Marijo had latched on to her the moment she'd climbed into the truck.

"He's a real hunk," Marijo was saying. "And a nice guy. That's a hard-to-beat and hard-to-find combination."

"True," Asia murmured.

She was unable to think of a way to turn the conversation back onto the other woman. She should be finding a way to make Marijo expose herself, but she couldn't think. Her brain was on information overload.

"So, are you two a serious item?"

"I'm not sure."

That was the truth. Though she was attracted to Dominic and was getting attached to him despite her reservations, Asia didn't know what could come of their relationship. They were in a special situation, after all. Once they'd accomplished their mission, they'd have no reason to stay together. Dominic would go his way, no doubt continuing to hide from his past. No matter how many times she told herself he'd had good reasons for making a new life for himself, she couldn't tolerate the thought of him giving up because things went haywire.

Even as she rationalized, a little voice argued that there could be more between them, that she was in fact letting one incident with a stranger stop her from realizing the full potential of a possible relationship with a man who could be good for her.

If only Dominic would get his head straight and regain pride in himself, that was.

Her thoughts on the subject scattered as the canteen truck rolled to a stop in a clearing.

"This is it," the head cook stated, jumping to the ground. "Everybody out and get busy."

"See you later," Marijo said.

Workers tumbled out of the back of the truck. Asia waited till last. "Thanks for the ride," she told the cook.

"No problem."

As the staff set up portable tables on which they would place bagged lunches, cold drinks, baskets of fresh fruits and trays of candies, Asia headed for the loading area where a tractor was hauling in a limbless tree.

"Have you seen Dominic Crawford?" she asked, raising her voice to be heard above the noise of not only nearby equipment engines, but the whine of saws in the distance.

The operator removed an earplug and leaned out of the cab. "What?"

"Dominic Crawford. Do you know where he is?"

"Got me, lady. Back in there somewhere," he stated, indicating the thick of the forest.

"Then you don't know how long it'll be before he gets back here?"

A worker in a blue plaid shirt said, "Probably not for a while. He brought a couple of logs in and went back for another. You just missed him. He'll be here for lunch for sure though."

Asia checked her watch. Another half hour. She couldn't tolerate standing around and waiting. And if Haskel showed, he'd want to know why she wasn't back at the employment office. Asia didn't relish having to explain herself until she'd talked to Dominic.

"Do you think I could find him myself if I followed this road?" she asked the man in blue plaid.

"Maybe. There's a shortcut through the woods," the guy said, pointing.

"Thanks."

Waving to the helpful man, Asia started up the rutted trail until she realized another tractor was inching its way down, hauling a load, raising a cloud of dust. She could choke to death by the time she waited for it to pass. Maybe she should take the shortcut.

With a last glance at the loading area where everyone seemed to be involved in their job rather than in her, Asia struck out into the woods.

Alone among giant pine and fir trees, the forest floor covered with a carpet of pine needles, Asia felt at peace within minutes. She headed toward the still-distant drone of saws and the resounding thumps that told her another tree had fallen. A natural path undoubtedly made by deer and other forest creatures led her farther from the road, but it was easier than struggling through the underbrush. It also led straight to a stream that was wider than she could cross without getting wet.

Her gaze followed the ribbon of clear gurgling water deeper into the dusky forest where the stream seemed to narrow. Because she didn't look forward to being stuck in wet shoes for the rest of the day, she followed the bank, hoping for an easier crossing. Intent on finding a narrow spot in the stream, Asia didn't realize how far she'd gone until she'd succeeded and had leaped to the other bank.

An owl skittered overhead, its hoot startling her.

She paused and strained to hear. Man-made noises were more distant. Muffled. Confusing.

And as Asia tried to sort out her direction, she thought she heard a footfall.

Her pulse lurched. Telling herself that all sizes of animals lived in the forest didn't stem her overactive imagination. Not when she so clearly remembered the dark street in Port Townsend that led to the beach.

Remembered the sense of unnamed danger that had engulfed her then.

Remembered the attack.

Asia's mouth went dry. Her heart pushed up into her throat, its beat loud in her ears. Instinct shoved her forward when she heard a splash directly behind her.

She panicked...ran blindly...not even knowing if she were headed in the right direction.

The gigantic trees seemed to close in on her. Peace turned to danger. The air was humid, as cloying as the curtain of moss hanging from a branch that hit her in the face. Her chest hurt with her effort, but on she went until a downed and rotting log hooked her ankle and tumbled her to the cushioned forest floor.

Something sharp impaled her hand—a dried twig that cracked under the weight of her fall. She pulled the remaining wood free, ignored the blood that welled and slid over her numb fingers. Her breath was coming in deep gasps and her limbs felt weak, but somehow she managed to push herself to her feet and continue on.

She stumbled forward, away from the danger behind her.

But how could she be sure what lay behind... ahead? Which direction was which?

Recognizing a familiar-looking broken-topped tree, a snag favored by owls, Asia realized she'd run in a circle. She forced herself to stop, to breathe deeply until her lungs were under control, until she could get her bearings. All the while, she scanned the shadows of the forest, piercing the dark emerald gloom with fright-filled eyes. She saw nothing coming after her. She heard nothing but the chain saws, closer now.

Imagination—or so she tried to tell herself with little success.

Asia pulled herself together and quickly headed toward the sound of human activity. She kept her head and continued to glance over her shoulder every few seconds. No one there now. Instinct rather than proof told her that she hadn't imagined the footfall or the splash—that someone rather than something had followed her. Maybe was following her still.

A distant thwack shuddered through the earth. More mechanical whines. She followed the sounds of men working, which grew even louder.

Another noise from behind pushed her forward into a thick copse. She stopped to get her bearings, to figure out which direction meant safety. Hushed footfalls stalked her, seemed to surround her.

And then—as if all human activity had ceased for a second by some universal agreement—silence filled the forest. Asia was confused until she heard the loud, obscene crack, recognized the excruciating groan.

It was a primal forest scream.

An ancient tree newly felled by man.

Asia whipped around, saw the death throes of the gigantic fir ten feet in diameter toppling toward her as if in slow motion. Recognizing her own imminent demise if it should catch up with her, she forced her muscles to respond to the danger, forced her legs to work. She tripped, then got to her feet and slipped on the damp undergrowth.

The tree was descending fast now. She heard its whoosh, felt its last gasp of breath wash over her as it came crashing down. She had barely moved out of range when the massive trunk collided with the forest floor that quaked beneath her feet.

She was safe!

But before Asia could catch her breath, a limb broke free and came flying at her, striking her on the side of the head. Unbearable pain brought her to her knees, to the brink of consciousness. Blackness striated with pinpoints of light sought to envelop her. She shook her head to clear it, yet felt herself fading to flee the agony.

Then she heard the footsteps coming closer.

Trapped—she was trapped! The murderer had an easy target. She couldn't fight any longer, had to give way...

"Hey, you all right?" A concerned male voice brought her back, struggling and trying not to cry out with the pain.

"Where the hell'd she come from?" asked another.

Slowly, so slowly, Asia opened her eyes as strong, gloved hands grasped the soft flesh of her upper arms. Confused, she looked from face to face, searching for one she knew. Searching for Dominic.

"What happened?" a woman asked.

"She popped out of nowhere just as we made the back cut," a man said. He nervously wiped his gloved hands on his red flannel shirt. "Almost bought the farm."

"Get her out of here, easy," came a voice of authority that belonged to the crew foreman. "Can't you see she needs medical attention?"

Asia opened her mouth to protest, to tell them she could walk if they gave her a minute. But looking beyond the workers crowding around her, she changed her mind when her gaze lighted on a familiar if expressionless face.

The face of Marijo Lunt.

Chapter Nine

Judge Jasper Raferty paced the length of his gloomy chambers. Unable to concentrate on the case he'd been hearing, he'd called an early recess. He couldn't concentrate on anything with the Crawley situation up in the air. He hadn't heard from Asia since she'd gone off with the kingpin's son. And he hadn't heard from the ex-con he'd sent after her since the afternoon before. All he knew for sure was that Asia was in Olympia Grove and working for a logging company.

What in the world did she think she was up to?

Didn't she realize what kind of danger she was in?

"Dear God, don't let Crawley succeed," Jasper muttered as he continued to pace. "Don't let him harm my daughter any more than he has."

Not only his daughter, his baby. The child of his heart. She was her mother reincarnated. A little more daring, perhaps, but no less loved.

The telephone shrilled him to a stop. And did the same with his breath.

He lifted the receiver and ground out, "Judge Raferty here."

"Judge, it's me."

Air sluiced into his lungs in a great rush. "Thank God. I thought you'd never call. Everything's all right, isn't it?" When he didn't get an instant response, he had trouble breathing again. And his left shoulder started to ache. "Is everything all right?"

"You daughter is safe for now."

"What do you mean for now?" Jasper asked, his voice shaky. "What's going on?"

"Crawley got to her."

"Tell me."

Jasper listened to details first about the fire, then the incident with the tree. His stomach knotted and his heart squeezed into a fist.

"You watch over her. You keep my baby safe," he begged. "I'll pay you anything."

Even if he had to sell what was left of the estate. His financial reverses had tempted him to take Crawley's bribe in the first place. Perhaps he should have gone through with the deal, forced down his guilt. Perhaps then his children would be safe.

"Listen, Judge," his contact was saying, "you did all right by me when I got out of stir. You called in a favor and I agreed to help you. Your kid doesn't deserve to die for scum like King Crawley. I'll do everything I can to keep her safe."

Jasper's hand was shaking by the time he replaced the receiver. The pain was getting worse. And his vision was starting to distort. His fingers clutched the edge of his desk.

"Not now," he groaned, damning himself for not having seen that doctor. "Dear God, not when my daughter needs me."

That devil's spawn was responsible for Asia's near accidents. Jasper was sure of it. His trusting child had walked right into the spider's web when she'd gone off with Dominic Crawford. He had to warn her himself. He had to get to Olympia Grove. He had to be around to protect all three of his children.

But as he took one step from his desk, Jasper crumpled and fell to the plush carpeted floor in agony. Reality came rushing in. He wasn't going anywhere.

Unless it was straight to hell.

HEART RACING, Dominic stopped the tractor in the parking lot, jumped down and ran to where several people gathered around Asia. Head hanging, torso barely upright, she sat on a bench in front of the first aid office.

"Here, put this ice pack on your head. It'll stop the swelling," the nurse said.

He shoved his way into the small crowd in time to see Asia as she took the offering with a bandaged hand. She didn't look as bad as he had feared. His heart had almost stopped when one of the men had told him she'd had an accident. He caught her staring at Marijo who hung back from the others, arms crossed over her chest. What was going on?

"What happened?" he asked Asia as she applied the ice pack to the side of her head.

"I got clipped by a flying branch. It left a great lump."

Marijo drew closer. "She was lucky the whole tree didn't get her. That was a close call."

"You were there?"

The redhead nodded. She seemed a bit uncomfortable when she told him, "I went for a walk to stretch my legs. I heard this commotion and there Asia was, sprawled out, trying to stay conscious.''

Sensing the tension emanating from the woman he loved, Dominic stooped to face her. ''We ought to get you to a hospital.''

''I don't need a hospital.'' She gave Marijo a sideways glance. ''Ice and a few extra-duty aspirins will do the trick.''

Dominic looked to the nurse for confirmation.

She shrugged and said, ''No signs of concussion. She's moving fine, if slowly. I think a couple of aspirins are in order. I'll get them.''

Dominic could hardly believe Asia had been battered yet again, and just when her old bruises were almost gone. Unable to ask her what had really happened—he didn't for a moment believe her almost being felled by a tree was a simple accident—he squeezed her free hand reassuringly.

A truck pulled up with a squeal of tires and Norman Haskel jumped out. ''All right, time to break up the socializing. Get lunch, then back to work,'' he ordered. ''I'll see to Miss Raferty.''

Grumbling, the workers did as they were told, reluctantly piling back into the crummy that had brought them down from the logging site. Only Dominic remained behind.

Standing, he told Haskel, ''She's going to take the rest of the day off.''

''She's going to take more than a day.'' Haskel's face was ruddy with anger. ''Miss Raferty, you're fired!''

''What?'' Dominic demanded with an indignant sputter. ''She gets hurt and you fire her?'' He attributed Asia's lack of anger to her weakened condition.

"She left her job. She was in charge of the office and she just walked out and left it."

"With Carol," Asia added. "But that's okay. Working for you is too dangerous."

"If you'd have stayed where you belonged—"

"Leave her be," Dominic interrupted.

"I don't believe this! I thought jobs were hard to come by. Nobody wants to do an honest day's work. Why are you here, Crawford? Didn't I tell you to get back to work? You belong up there," he said, pointing toward the logging site.

"If she doesn't work for you, neither do I."

Haskel stared with his mouth open.

"That's okay, Dom," Asia said, giving him a nudge of significance. "Working for him is problematic anyway. The *last* girl left after only a week."

Dominic stared. She wasn't making idle conversation. She had to mean Peggy. So the woman had worked here. And now she was gone, one step ahead of them. Asia must have gotten the information from the computer file. That's why she was letting Haskel fire her without an argument.

"Considering how unreliable Peggy was, I don't know why she thinks she'll be happier at another logging company," Haskel muttered as he stalked off and into his office.

"Here you are." The nurse returned with the aspirins and a glass of water. "Drink it all," she said.

Dominic took the ice pack from Asia and she obediently did as she was told. Another truck pulled into the lot while she was finishing the water. Distracted, the nurse didn't see Asia holding out the glass to her. She appeared a bit flustered.

"Hiya, Lenore," called a male voice. "Thought we could have lunch together today."

Dominic turned to see a guy in a blue plaid shirt approaching, two paper bags in one hand, two apples in the other.

"Sure, Mike," the nurse said. "Give me a minute to freshen up and get a blanket. We can eat under the trees."

As she went back into her office, the man looked from Dominic to Asia. "I see you found each other. The hard way. Now I'm sorry I told you about the shortcut. I figured you knew your way around a logging site."

"I went looking for you," Asia explained to Dominic.

And Dominic sensed she wanted to tell him more, but she couldn't while the man was there.

She turned to Mike. "Haskel fired me. I think the last woman who worked at my job set him off about what he considers irresponsible behavior."

"Yeah, he wasn't too happy when Peg left. She just up and walked away, leaving him with a load of extra work."

"For a better job, right? He said something about another timber company."

"I guess. Said she was going to join a good friend who told her about a company that was hiring in the Cascades."

"Do you know which one? We're both out of a job," she said, indicating Dominic as well.

Dominic couldn't believe Asia was quick-witted enough to do some detective work even with her brain scrambled. And he wondered who this "good friend" was. Could it be Jess? A rush of excitement pumped through him as he imagined Peggy leading them straight to his sister.

"Hmm, wish I could remember the name of the company." Mike's brow furrowed. "Something Forestry Products. Best I can do. Sorry."

"Maybe if you tell us where she's staying, we can ask her ourselves."

"Peggy already left town. She hitched a ride on my flatbed when I hauled a load of lumber into Aberdeen first thing yesterday morning."

Just before they'd arrived, no doubt, Dominic thought. He asked, "She doesn't have a car?"

Mike shook his head. "Rides the rails. Don't cost nothing, you know. Hoboes do it all the time. Actually, a lot of workers along the West Coast do the same."

Dominic was fully aware that migrant workers, unable to pay for transportation because of low salaries, used this method to get from job to job. While hoboing wasn't legal, the authorities usually turned a blind eye to the situation as long as there was no trouble. Wise move since the economy of the region would suffer even more if farmers had to pay higher wages. Either product prices would rise or all but the conglomerates would be forced out of business.

"Thanks for the information," Dominic told the trucker. "Maybe we can find the name of the company in the Yellow Pages. We'll just call any outfit located in the Cascades with 'Forestry Products' as part of the name."

"Clever guy," Mike said, giving him the thumbs-up sign.

Just then the nurse exited her office, a blanket under her arm. "I'm ready, Mike." She locked the door behind her. "You'll be all right until you get a ride back to town, won't you?" she asked Asia.

"My head's feeling better already."

"Good. Any problems, have your friend here give me a yell and I'll come running."

"Good luck finding another job," Mike said, taking Lenore's arm and leading her toward a copse of trees.

Dominic sat on the bench next to Asia. "We'll have to wait awhile—at least until lunch is over and one of the trucks leaves with a full load. Might be another half hour. Think you can hang in there?"

"I don't see that I have much choice," Asia said, lowering the ice bag. "I don't think Haskel's going to be offering us any free rides into town."

"Maybe I should threaten him with a lawsuit—"

"No. Leave it. I'll sit here for as long as I have to."

"Whatever possessed you to come looking for me?" Dominic asked, his concern turning to anger as he thought about the danger she'd put herself in. His heart had practically stopped when he'd heard about the accident. Horrible visions had haunted him as he'd guided the tractor down from the loading area. "I thought we agreed that you'd stay here where you'd be safe."

"After I learned Peggy was gone? And Jessica?"

"What?"

"Your sister worked here for several months, until a few weeks ago. She and Peggy had the same references, so I'll bet anything the 'good friend' who told her about the new job was—"

"Jess. I thought that myself. We're going to find her!" Then he sobered. "If anything had happened to you . . ." Dominic's throat closed as he thought about this beautiful woman, the woman he loved, crushed beneath a mammoth tree. "I mean anything serious—"

"You'd what?"

"I would have blamed myself. I should have made you go back to Seattle."

Asia tensed. "Don't start that again. Don't treat me like an incompetent child. I've had enough of that from my father."

"I want to treat you like someone I care about, damn it!" Dominic practically shouted. Realizing what he'd almost admitted to her—and that they didn't need anyone else apprised of what they were about—he lowered his voice. "Forget I said that."

"I don't want to forget it, not if you meant it. I'd rather hear more."

"No. It's impossible." He was trying to be realistic. "I'm a Crawley and you're a Raferty."

"No, you're your own man and I'm my own woman," Asia countered. "That's all that really matters. Forget who our families are."

"Can you really forget what my father has done to your family?"

"I'll never forget the horrible things King Crawley orchestrated. But you're not your father. I don't hold you responsible for his actions."

Wiser in the ways of the world than she, he knew Asia was looking at the situation wearing blinders. They were attracted to each other, true, and she was drawn to him by the sense of danger that surrounded them, but she couldn't feel about him the way he did her. He had reason to love her because of her strength and compassion and absolute loyalty. On the other hand, he remembered how she'd told him off that first day; and he was the same man she'd disrespected then.

"You only say you don't hold me responsible now," Dominic said, "because we've been made allies by our unusual circumstances."

"I say that because I judge a man by who he is and what he does. I don't care who your father is."

"You *will* care," he insisted. "You're fooling yourself if you think differently. Someday you'll be sorry you had anything to do with me."

Asia stared at him wide-eyed for a moment. He hated her expression, which he interpreted as pitying. When she spoke, she did so with hesitancy, as if she were afraid of opening an old wound.

"She must have hurt you deeply."

The switch in topic tightened Dominic's jaw. While he thought of himself as healed, he also knew the scars of memory would remain forever. He didn't want to think about the way Priscilla had so easily abandoned him when the going got rough. He certainly didn't want to talk about her.

"Don't judge me by what your ex-wife did to you, Dom, please," Asia said.

He didn't miss her continued use of the nickname Jess had given him. It made him think she had some real affection for him. As if she sensed him softening his stand, she slipped a hand over his, made him want to forgo any more arguments and take her in his arms.

"Give me the same benefit of the doubt as I give you," she pleaded.

But Dominic knew he couldn't. He wouldn't willingly put himself through torture he could prevent. Asia had a good heart, but entering into a more complex, more intimate relationship with her would never work. Having her for a short while only to lose her forever might destroy him completely. He pulled his hand free and tried to ignore the immediate hurt so visible in her lovely face.

A logging truck rumbling down the access road gave him a respite from an uncomfortable subject. Warning Asia to stay put, he jogged to the crossing and flagged the driver. The man brought the flatbed to a stop and on request agreed to take them back to town.

They crowded into the cab, Asia in the middle. The radio blared all the way, preventing the necessity for small talk—something Dominic could be thankful for. By the time they got to the trailer park, he had a grip on himself. He helped her down out of the cab and thanked the driver.

As they walked toward their trailer, the conversation turned to an equally serious topic when Asia told him what she'd learned about their suspects by going through the computer files.

"So all three of them lied," he said. "Why aren't I surprised?"

"Only one of them is after us, though," Asia said logically. "We can probably eliminate Yerkes since at least one of his supposed employers checked out."

Dominic wasn't quick to agree. "The more recent reference covering the past several years was a phony."

"So you don't think we should eliminate him as a possible suspect?"

"Do you?"

Appearing distressed, she said, "I guess you're right. It wouldn't pay to be off guard the way I was this morning." She explained, "I think one of them was following me."

"You mean through the woods?"

Asia nodded. "I heard footsteps that weren't in my imagination. And then...after I was almost flattened into a pancake by the tree, I spotted Marijo. She was standing back, watching. She looked guilty."

Wondering if Marijo had been knowledgeable enough to purposely drive Asia into danger, he asked, "Are you sure you didn't mean horrified?"

"Her expression was strange, whatever she was thinking. But would she have been there at all if not to follow me? Considering she was supposed to be working lunch, her story about stretching her legs bothers me."

"And the matches bother me," Dominic added. When she gave him a questioning look, he said, "I never got around to telling you I found a book of matches outside the trailer after the fire. It was from Tully's Tap and Grill."

Asia frowned. "Eddy was the one we saw there."

"But Marijo used matches from the place yesterday when she lighted a cigarette."

"Is it really possible your father would have sent a woman to do his dirty work?"

"With King Crawley, anything is possible."

Having arrived at the trailer, Dominic unlocked the door and checked the premises before letting Asia enter.

"No one here but us." As she stepped inside, holding on to the door frame for support, he realized she still wasn't steady on her feet. He wondered how clear her memory was. "You wouldn't know who was logging the tree that almost got you?"

"Not really. Some guy in a red flannel shirt said I surprised them, so he must have been one of the men."

"The only guy I saw wearing red flannel was Yerkes's partner."

"Oh, my God." She sagged against the counter of the tiny kitchen area. "And Yerkes could have been the one to make the cut. We know he had the experience to do so. What if Marijo followed me there and got me in position to be hurt?" Her fingers worried the countertop. "Now I'm reaching, but figuring this out might be impossible, at least until it's too late."

Dominic wanted to promise that he wouldn't let anything happen to her, but the near miss told him how ineffectual his vows were—and made him want to stay by her side every single minute. But there was research to be done and he could tell Asia needed some rest.

"Why don't you lie down while I go over to MacGregor's to make a couple of telephone calls," he suggested. "I want to track down that forestry company, maybe check on the train schedules. We're going after Peggy as soon as possible. If we're lucky, she'll lead us right to Jess. I'll be back soon."

Asia merely nodded and went into the bedroom where she crawled onto the bed fully clothed. "I'll be waiting," she muttered into a pillow.

Once he got to work on the telephone, it didn't take him long to track down two companies in the Cascade Mountains with names similar to the one Mike was trying to remember—Washington Forest Product Industries and Pacific Forestry Products. Only the latter had job openings, so that had to be the one.

After settling that in his mind, he went to the window and scoped out the trailer park to make sure no one was sneaking around presenting further threat to Asia.

Satisfied, he next checked on the freight trains leaving Aberdeen for Klamoth Bend, Oregon, home to Pacific Forestry Products. This was more complex because there was nothing direct to the small mountain town. He was getting anxious by the time he secured all the needed information.

"You leaving Mountain Timber already?" Sandy asked from behind the counter.

Realizing the clerk had overheard his conversation, Dominic hedged, "Afraid I've been fired," and hoped that she hadn't figured out exactly where he was going.

"Too bad." She shrugged and went back to work restocking the floor-to-ceiling refrigerator with cans of beer and soda. "Happens to the best of them."

Dominic checked over his notes. Peggy would have had to change in Tacoma, then again in Portland. Since she was freight-hopping, the earliest she could have left Aberdeen for Tacoma in a boxcar was on a late-night or early-morning train. And considering freights picked up and left off cars at nearly every major stop, the going wouldn't be fast. Added to the ordinary interruptions, once in Tacoma, Peggy would have to get across town to another yard to pick up the next freight. That meant she didn't have a big lead on them.

A preoccupied Dominic stuffed the notebook into a jeans pocket as a plan gelled in his mind. He was mulling over the details and heading for the door until an insistent hand caught at his arm.

"Dominic, I asked how Asia was."

Startled, he stopped in his tracks and whipped around to see Marijo standing there, staring at him expectantly. Since he hadn't seen her, he wondered for how long. And, more important, how much had she heard?

"Asia's resting," he finally said.

"Good. A blow on the head like that isn't something to fool around with."

Marijo looked convincingly concerned, but Dominic wasn't going to give anyone the benefit of the doubt from now on. Not until they were out of the line of fire.

"Don't worry, she'll be fine." Dominic backed toward the door. "See you later."

Without making further excuses, he left the building, glancing back only once to see Marijo staring after him. Certain her interest wasn't casual, he jogged to the trailer to make sure he hadn't lied about Asia's being all right.

She was sound asleep.

Time was of the essence, but he didn't have the heart to wake her until he absolutely had to. He packed his few things, then started on hers. Asia stirred and groaned.

A hand went to her head as she squinched open her eyes and croaked, "What's going on?"

"We're leaving."

"For where?"

"We've got a train to catch."

Dominic ducked into the bathroom and stuffed her toiletries into the top of her overnight bag. Then he grabbed his shaving kit and strode into the living room.

A groggy Asia staggered out of the bedroom. "Wait, I want to get cleaned up."

"We don't have time. Besides, you look appropriate for the situation." Grubby. But beautiful. "Splash some water on your face and let's get going."

"What train?" she asked. "You mean in Aberdeen?"

"Tacoma."

Where they would join the ranks of hoboes who rode the rails free, Dominic thought, dropping the shaving kit into his duffel bag. And if they were lucky, they would catch up to Peggy *before* she arrived in Klamoth Bend.

STILL A LITTLE WOOZY and headachy from being whacked nearly senseless, Asia didn't realize Marijo was waiting for her until she got to the Bronco.

"Hi," the redhead said, stepping out from under the shade of a pine. "You're not looking too bad for a woman who tangled with a tree, thank goodness." She paused only a second before adding, "I, uh, guessed you'd be leaving."

Asia stiffened and took a fast look around. They were alone. Dominic had gone back into the trailer for her shoulder bag, which she'd forgotten she'd shoved under the bed.

"Haskel didn't give us much choice," she said faintly, even as she wondered what the other woman wanted and silently begged Dominic to hurry.

"Firing you was a creepy thing to do after what happened, but maybe it was for the best." Marijo gave her an abashed grin. "You're not the only one who didn't work out. I decided not to stick around, either. That's why I'm here. I was wondering if I could hitch a ride with you."

Fingers of fear closed around Asia's throat, making it difficult for her to speak. "Uh, I don't know."

"Please." The grin faded. "I can't stay here. I've got to get away from Eddy. He's too friendly, if you know what I mean."

"What?"

"He's been coming on to me at every opportunity. Well, more than coming on." Marijo peeled back her long-sleeved shirt to show Asia her wrist. "He did this. He's tried to get me alone several times. I have to get away from here before he has another opportunity to hurt me."

Seeing Marijo's bruises made Asia's stomach clench. Her recent attack was still too fresh in her mind to let her ignore this and see to her own interests. If they helped Marijo, she didn't have to know exactly where they were headed.

"We could give you a lift into the next town," she offered, albeit reluctantly.

"I suppose that's better than nothing. It's just that . . . I'm afraid he'll catch up to me."

"You can get another ride."

"Yeah, maybe. If I can find another woman or a couple who'll take me. I have to get all the way to Tacoma. I want to go home." Marijo wet her lips. "Please, you're a woman. You said you've hitched before. You know what it can be like. Please."

The redhead had a convincing edge to her voice that chilled Asia. She couldn't turn her back on the other woman's plight. A door slamming alerted her that Dominic was leaving the trailer.

"Let me talk to Dominic," she said, quickly moving toward him and pulling him aside.

In a low voice, she repeated Marijo's request and her reason for wanting to agree.

"Are you crazy?" he whispered.

"I don't know. Maybe. But Eddy has been bugging her. I saw him with my own eyes. And he gives me the creeps."

Dominic enfolded her shoulders with gentle hands. "Think about this. You told me yourself Marijo might have been the one following you."

"I could have been wrong. Or maybe she was taking a shortcut to the logging site like I was, not following me at all. What if we leave her behind and something happens to her? I couldn't live with myself, Dom. Let's take her to Tacoma and be careful we don't let her know where we're going from there. Okay?"

"All right," he agreed, though he looked distinctly unhappy.

Relieved, Asia nodded and hoped she wasn't walking right into even more danger with her eyes wide open.

Chapter Ten

On the route to Tacoma, Marijo kept up such a lively stream of chatter from the back seat that Asia began to wonder whether or not it was purposeful. Was the redhead trying to distract them from coming up with reasons other than the one she gave for her tagging along?

Asia would be glad when they parted company and she and Dominic could concentrate on finding Peggy without a shadow. Surely this time they would be safe.

"So, where are you two headed after Tacoma?" Marijo asked when they were a few miles from their destination.

Dominic said, "Seattle."

"Seattle." With an amused laugh, she teased, "And you really think you'll be able to find work logging there."

"We thought we'd take a vacation," Asia said, wondering if the redhead really expected them to be truthful. Then, again, she might not have any ulterior motives at all. "We're going to visit family for a while."

Dominic slowed the truck and turned into a combination filling station and grocery store. "I'll get gas and some food to take along on the ride."

"Great," Marijo said. "I could use the facilities."

As could Asia, who followed the other woman into the ladies' room.

After freshening up, she got a glimpse of herself in the mirror. How pale she looked. To make herself feel better, she dug through her shoulder bag until she found a tube of lipstick. But after swiping her lips with a bright coral, Asia realized the stuff looked kind of silly when Dominic hadn't given her time to clean up properly or apply a cover-up to the fading bruises before they left the trailer park. Her face looked as smudged as her T-shirt.

At the next sink, Marijo muttered to herself as she searched through her backpack. "Now where is that comb?" Triumphant, she pulled it out and attacked her tangle of spiked hair, then gave a discouraged moan. "I don't even know why I bothered. I made it look worse."

Turning to inspect the other woman's hair more directly, Asia froze when her gaze lighted on the fancy comb in Marijo's hand. An antique, it was edged with silver and all too familiar.

Marijo suddenly realized Asia was staring with something akin to shock. "What's wrong?"

"Where did you get that?" Asia asked, her gaze sweeping up to the other woman's face.

"Pretty, isn't it?" But the redhead's nervous expression belied her casual words. "This was a gift—from Eddy. Why?"

"I had one exactly like it. Mine was stolen."

"You don't think I..." Marijo didn't finish the query. Instead she held out the comb and said, "Here, if it is yours, take the damn thing."

Asia did so and silently inspected the design in the silver. She recognized a small scratch in the soft metal as being one she'd made accidentally.

"It's mine all right."

"Eddy said he found it outside of MacGregor's. You must have dropped it."

Now that was impossible, not that Asia told her so. She merely stared at Marijo. The other woman seemed to be having difficulty keeping an even gaze.

And no wonder.

The comb had been in Asia's purse the night she'd been attacked. The purse that had been stolen. So how had the comb ended up outside of MacGregor's? Did Yerkes drop it so Eddy could find it? Or did Eddy lie about finding it in the first place? Or was Marijo the liar?

Maybe the redhead was connected to the man who'd attacked Asia—a possible stranger she had not yet met face-to-face in the light.

Not saying a word, she stuffed the comb into her shoulder bag, stalked out of the ladies' room and toward the Bronco. Marijo followed and climbed into the back as Dominic arrived, arms around a paper bag filled with food. If he sensed anything was wrong, he didn't ask, merely slid behind the wheel and drove the remaining few miles to Tacoma.

In the heart of the downtown area, at the edge of the pedestrian mall, he pulled over to let Marijo out.

"Thanks," she said, reaching in for her backpack. Then, as if she were trying to make up her mind about something, she chose not to move away so Asia could close the door on her. "Listen, Asia, about the comb—"

"You explained how you got it, didn't you? There's nothing more to say."

"Yeah, there is—if you'll let me. I didn't steal it, I swear. Can we go somewhere for coffee—"

But Asia cut her off again with an abrupt, "I'm not thirsty. Goodbye, Marijo."

As if sensing Asia wasn't going to give, Marijo stepped back from the vehicle, but continued to stare at Asia through troubled eyes. Dominic took off and kept going until he'd put a respectable distance between them. Then he pulled the truck over once again.

Turning to Asia, he said, "Let's have it. What was going on back there?"

She took the comb out of her purse and showed it to him. "We may have been played for a couple of fools." Quickly explaining, she added, "I can't wait to get on the rails. Traveling as a hobo seems safe compared to what we've been doing for the past few days." A view she hadn't at first taken when he'd revealed his plan.

"No one should be able to find us now," Dominic said.

And yet Asia heard the doubt in his words. A doubt that chilled her because it matched her own. What if the would-be murderer knew their every move? Rather than providing them with the safety they were looking for, would the final leg of their journey prove to be the end of their lives?

KING CRAWLEY TRIED to keep his face a blank when he entered the familiar dank room, but was afraid he couldn't hide his shock at seeing Sydney Raferty waiting for him. He hadn't figured on her being the mysterious visitor. To cover, he gave her an evil smile meant to intimidate as he took the chair on the other side of the table.

She didn't react.

Instead her gaze met his directly, her pale eyes giving her a fey look...and giving him the creeps. He felt as though those eyes could bore right through him and peer around his rotting soul.

He struck out at her the only way he could, with words and an unbending attitude. "You got me outta my bunk, baby doll, so talk."

She had the guts to take her own sweet time, he'd give her that. She waited until he was squirming inside. Crawley hated the unfamiliar uncertainty of not being in charge of a situation, but his curiosity was piqued.

"I wanted to meet the man who has so much hate in his heart that he would do anything to destroy three people he's never even met."

Relief exploded through his barrel chest and erupted into a bubble of laughter. "If that's all..." Flattening his hands against the table's surface, he started to rise.

"Sit, Mr. Crawley. I'm not through with you."

Her soft voice shot a chill down his spine. Her tone was rich with the power of knowledge. Despite his urgency to escape this room, to escape her, he dropped back to the chair. While the chill spread over his body, he didn't give her the benefit of seeing anything but the hardened criminal he was.

"I don't like my time being wasted."

"That's right. You don't have much time left, do you," she said frankly if not quite cruelly. "Can't you think of a productive way to spend your last days—like atoning for your crimes against humanity?''

''You make my heart bleed, baby doll.''

''Do you have a heart? What would it take to make you feel something other than this destructive hate that's eating away at you? My father is hospitalized, in intensive care because of you, but I'm sure you know that.''

''I do,'' he said, not without satisfaction.

''He may never recover to see the fruits of your one-sided vendetta,'' she said, her voice quivering with emotion for a moment. But then she got hold of herself. ''So what good is going through with your plan if the man you wanted to see suffer never knows of its success?''

''*I'll* know and that's what counts.''

''Haven't you gotten your fill of vengeance yet?'' she demanded, raising her voice for the first time. ''Kenneth Lord is dead because of you. I was almost killed more than once. My brother could have been killed as well. A little child was brutally separated from her mother. She wakes up screaming in the middle of the night. Who knows how long it will take her to get over the nightmares—''

''Enough!'' he shouted. ''These people mean nothing to me. *You* mean nothing—''

''But your son does.''

Dead silence. Her very certainty sent Crawley mentally reeling, even as he tried to figure out what she was talking about. She knew she had him. He couldn't ignore her and leave as he wanted. He had to ask.

''What's Dominic got to do with any of this?''

''I thought your informants were the best.''

Something about the way she was looking at him made Crawley want to run out of the room. Pity. That's what he saw in her eyes, in her expression. And more. She had a power, this one. He'd thought her nondescript and ineffectual, but he was finding Sydney Raferty far stronger than he'd given her credit for. Stronger than he was. She made him want to hide from what she would say next. But he sensed the kid trick wouldn't keep her from zeroing in on him.

"Last night I had a dream...a vision." Sydney turned inward and her voice went odd as she forestalled his protest. "You're usually a thorough man, Mr. Crawley. You know about my gifts."

"What do you mean *usually?* And if you got something to tell me about Dominic, do it and get outta here!"

"They were on a train and in great danger."

"They? Who's *they?*"

She spoke as if she hadn't heard him, merely went on in that odd fashion of hers. "They were searching for Jess."

"Jess? What are you talking about? My daughter is dead."

Her eyes cleared, seared him with their intensity. "No, she's not. Not yet."

"What the hell are you talking about?" he repeated.

Was it possible that his sweet Jessica was still alive?

"Your son and my sister are trying to find her together."

"You're crazy."

"Am I?" She didn't wait for his response. "In my vision, Dominic and Asia were searching the train cars for Jess. Not on a passenger train—but on the kind that hauls freight. Only they weren't alone. I felt a menace, a horrible presence. Evil. And I felt your son's pain."

"No, this can't—"

She rode over his protest. "A pain so searing as to be almost unbearable. And blood. I couldn't see exactly what happened, but there was a struggle and a lot of blood, Mr. Crawley. Dominic was covered with it. Maybe too much blood for him to survive."

Crawley's stomach clenched and a ham-sized fist squeezed at his chest so he had trouble breathing. "You really are wacko."

"Maybe I am. But if I were you, I would think about this: you didn't even know Dominic was with my sister. How could you have told your assassin to make sure no harm came to your son? And even if you gave those orders now, do you think Dominic would stand by and watch another human being die? Especially a woman he loves? Surely you know your son better than that. He'd try to protect her with his own life."

"This is a trick!" Crawley yelled, shooting upright. "You've made up this elaborate story because you wanna see me suffer."

"Not I, Mr. Crawley. The irony is that you're responsible for your own suffering." Sighing, she stood. "I've warned you. Now it's up to you to act. You hold the fate of your own children as well as my family in your hands. If you don't do something to stop this insanity, you'll never see your daughter again, and Dominic's death will be on your conscience."

With that, Sydney Raferty moved to the guard who opened the door for her. She left without looking back.

Crawley stared after her, unable to move, his body suddenly coated with sweat. He'd been told Asia Rafferty was traveling with a man, but he'd been given no name. What if this guy really was Dominic? What if Sydney really had seen this vision? And what if he, King Crawley, really was responsible for his own son's death?

What was he going to do now? What could he do? It was too damn late. They'd left the logging town for parts unknown. And they weren't alone.

He had no way to make contact.

God help him, he couldn't stop the killing machine he'd set in motion.

All he could do was wait.

HAVING LEFT THE BRONCO on a nearby side street, Dominic and Asia made their way toward the railroad yard. They'd had a large if unsatisfying fast-food dinner that would keep them from being hungry too soon, and in their bags, they'd packed the snack food he'd bought in the gas station. They were ready to roll, if only they could get into the yard surrounded by an old and rusting six-foot chain-link fence without being seen by someone who might take exception to their presence. It would be dark soon, at which time they would be able to move around more freely.

A block or so down, Dominic spotted a break where the chain link had pulled away from its post. He figured the rent was large enough for them to crawl through into the switching yard. He pulled the loose fencing aside, providing a gap approximately three feet high by two wide.

"Plenty of room."

"For a kid."

Despite her protest, Asia threw her overnight bag to the other side, then scrambled through the opening on hands and knees. She took Dominic's duffel bag from him and moved out of the way as he came after her with a bit more difficulty because of his larger size.

"Do you know what you're doing?" she asked as he got to his feet.

"I hopped freights a couple of times in my checkered youth," he admitted, looking around. More than a dozen sets of tracks lay between them and the other side of the yard where a control tower and a few buildings stood. "We need to get to the dispatch office so we can find out what time the next freight is leaving for Portland."

"You mean someone there will just give us the information, even though we're not paying customers?"

"Depends on the person and on the given railroad's policy. Some dispatchers are pretty friendly and helpful as long as the hoboes don't start trouble for them."

Dominic led the way, noting the track numbers painted on the switches. Putting a protective arm around Asia, he kept his eyes peeled for trouble, whether in the form of a threatening train or person.

Not only was he keeping an eye out for the yard bull who might enjoy exerting his authority for the hell of it, but for anyone who might mean Asia harm, as well. He could have sworn he'd spotted the same light-colored pickup more than one since they'd left Olympia Grove, first on the road, then in Tacoma. The person who'd tried to run Asia down? Though someone might be following them, he hadn't told her in hopes of giving her temporary peace of mind.

Once on the other side of the switching yard, Dominic turned to the sound of clacking. A boxcar came whooshing downhill and slowed on a distant track. A few seconds later, another followed and stopped on a track somewhat closer.

"Train's being humped," Dominic explained. "Cars are being uncoupled and switched to different trains by rolling them downhill."

"Sounds like a complicated system."

"A time-consuming one, anyway. Only the hotshots are on the same tight schedules as passenger trains. Most are slower. Let's go look for the switchman. He'll pretty much know what's going on in his yard."

He indicated the hill and they hurried to the top. The switchman wasn't difficult to find. As they approached the train being humped, a man in grimy overalls was bending over a coupling. Dominic waited until the old-fashioned refrigerated reefer car was released and went sailing downhill. Then he pressed Asia forward and approached.

"Excuse me, but can we talk to you a minute?" he called over the din.

The switchman straightened. He was a young guy, not more than twenty-five. He gave them the once-over but must have decided they were okay, because he said, "Yeah, sure, as long as you don't take too long. I gotta get this train broken up fast. So what is it?"

"We're looking for a woman," Asia said. "Early twenties, medium height, a little on the thin side, light brown hair, glasses."

"Hmm, I do remember a woman who fits the description—except for the glasses."

Asia looked up at Dominic. "Maybe Peggy doesn't wear them all the time."

"Could be."

"She was traveling alone." The switchman shook his head and strode the length of the open-topped gondola to the next coupling with Dominic and Asia right behind him. "Not safe for a pretty thing like her. Hoboing alone isn't safe for any woman," he said, giving Asia a significant look of warning. "You remember that."

"How long ago did you see her?" Dominic asked.

"This afternoon." Signaling to his partner who was farther down the tracks, he bent over to undo the coupling. "She got on a train headed to Sacramento."

"Did it by any chance stop in Portland?"

"Yep."

"That's got to be her, then," Dominic told Asia, his heart beating faster when her face brightened with hope. This was the way he wanted to see her first thing in the morning, last thing at night. Reluctantly he turned back to the switchman as the gondola clacked down the tracks. "When's the next train through Portland?"

"Sometime late tonight," the switchman said. "I'm off shift when I get done here, so I don't exactly know when. Sorry."

"Thanks. You've been a big help."

"Dispatch is the ugly gray building just before you get to the control tower."

The switchman waved his hand in the right direction before setting off for the next coupling.

Less than ten minutes later, Dominic and Asia arrived at the worn building the friendly switchman had indicated. A small sign over the doorway identified it as the Dispatch Office. He peered through the windows into a furnished but empty space.

"No one home, but let's see if the store is secured." The knob turned under his hand, so Dominic opened the door.

Directly behind him, Asia said, "Couldn't we be arrested for breaking and entering or something?"

"The place wasn't locked up. Besides, if anyone catches us in here, we're simply going to keep our heads and be polite."

Good advice. For no sooner did he get near the dispatch blackboard, on which train and track number, destination and departure time were listed, than the door creaked open.

"Hey, what are you two doing here?" asked a white-haired man with an unfriendly expression.

Next to him, Asia jumped. "We just wanted to take a look at your board," she returned in a friendly manner.

Dominic continued to scan the various destinations. Bellingham. Aberdeen. Boise. Los Angeles. Bingo! That was at least in the right direction, and it was scheduled to leave around eleven.

"Vagrants! Hoboes!" the elderly man yelled. He trudged to his desk where he put one hand on the telephone. "Get outta here before I sic the yard bull on your backs."

"But we weren't hurting anything, sir," Asia protested sweetly. "We're just trying to get to my sister before she has the baby."

Startled by the renewal of the tall tale, which changed with every telling, Dominic glanced away from the board for a second. Still smiling, Asia shoved a sharp elbow in his side and gave him the covert signal to keep reading. He found another train scheduled to leave for Salem, Oregon just before midnight and a third to Medford at two-twenty.

"We don't want to cause trouble for anyone," Asia was saying, "but you know how it is when someone you love needs you, right?"

The grumpy man wouldn't be won over. "I know your type. You just want something for nothing—a free ride—don't you? Two healthy youngsters like you should be able to pay your own way. When I was your age . . . ah, never mind. Get the heck out of here!"

"You won't have us arrested or anything, will you?"

Asia continued blathering as Dominic mentally memorized the three possible departures that would stop in Portland. But the dispatcher was obviously in no mood to be hornswoggled, though he didn't threaten them with the railroad police again.

"Just go and don't let me see your faces again!"

"We're on our way," Dominic said, sweeping Asia through the office to the door.

The creeping gray of deep twilight spread over the railroad yard when they exited. Removing his arm from her back, Dominic looked around for other workers who might be of help.

"What did you get?" Asia asked.

"Three possibles. The first one leaves for L.A. at eleven. That might or might not stop in Portland, but either or both of the later trains to Salem and Medford will."

"How are you going to find out about the L.A. train?"

"Ask."

Dominic spotted a yard worker on his way to the hill. They jogged to catch up to the guy and learned that they would have to catch the train to Salem, after all.

"We have a couple of hours to kill," Asia said. "Should we go somewhere for a while and come back?"

"We might as well stay around here," Dominic said. Easier to spot someone who didn't belong—the pickup was still on his mind. "It takes at least an hour, usually more to make up a freight. If we stick around, we can scope out the situation, see if there are any empties."

"So what do you propose doing until then?"

"Wait. We passed a shanty at the bottom of the hill that looked like it wasn't being used. The switchmen will probably be kept too busy to use it until we're gone. Let's check it out."

To Dominic's surprise, Asia slipped her hand in his as they walked toward the small dark building. Her touch burned through his defenses, made him too aware of what he wanted...and what he couldn't have. But no matter how many times he reminded himself of that, he couldn't help the longing. Despite their differences, he felt closer to Asia than he did to anyone.

As if she sensed what he was thinking, she gave his hand a squeeze. "This must be so difficult for you. Having to deal with unpleasant things instigated by your father."

Instigated? That was putting the case mildly. Dominic didn't bother denying he had a father as he might have done only days before. What he said was, "This is difficult for both of us."

"You still love him, don't you?"

"Don't push."

"Once a pest, always a pest. Admit it, Dominic. You love King Crawley."

"I couldn't love someone who was responsible for other people's deaths."

"But you love the man who was a special father to you for a lot of years," Asia countered.

To Dominic's relief, she dropped the subject as they drew near the shanty. He checked the place out through the single grimy window. No sign of life, but he knocked anyway. When there was no answer, he opened the unlocked door and found the light switch. A naked low-watt bulb cut through the dark blanketing the room, barely illuminating its unrelieved shabbiness.

"Coast is clear," he told Asia, slipping the straps of the purse and overnight bag from her shoulder. He set them and his duffel bag next to the doorway. "Not exactly cozy, but at least we can sit for a while."

He closed the door behind Asia who seemed too wound up to relax. She paced the small room with its ancient desk, two chairs, old-fashioned potbellied stove and a corner cot shrouded with a moth-eaten wool blanket. She seemed so agitated that Dominic began to wonder if she'd noticed anything out of the ordinary, like a familiar pickup or a face they might recognize from the logging company.

He didn't expect her to pick up the conversation about his father where she'd left it.

"Don't give yourself too hard a time over your feelings for your father anymore, okay?" she urged. "Try to separate the good from the bad, the way I had to do when I found out about my own."

He leaned back against the desk. "Our situations aren't exactly comparable."

"No, they're not. I guess I'll never know exactly how you feel. No one can."

"Except Jess, maybe."

Asia stopped her pacing and crossed to him. "We're going to find her, Dominic, believe that. We're getting closer. I'm certain Peggy Shield will lead us right to your sister."

"That's some confidence."

Her expression vulnerable, she said, "I have to believe nothing too terrible to bear will happen to me . . . even if I have to manipulate fate."

Dominic couldn't help reaching out to touch her. He smoothed the fall of hair back from her face, stroked her cheek with the callused pad of his thumb, slid his hand around the curve of her neck. She responded by rubbing the side of her head against him, placing her own hand on his chest. The bruises were mere smudges that now blended with the shadows of the dimly lighted room, the cut an angry scar that would fade with time.

Perhaps because he knew their quest was almost at an end, he couldn't get his fill of her. Her face was perfection with its barely slanted gray blue eyes, arched dark brows and the tiny mole at the left corner of a luscious mouth. Her lips parted as though she knew what he wanted to do to them.

"You're a plucky woman," he said softly.

"Plucky?" she whispered, swaying toward him. "I thought I was pesty."

"That, too. Pesty...pushy...plucky...and pretty." At the last, she made a choked sound. He smiled. "All right, beautiful."

"I wasn't fishing."

"That was an unsolicited testimonial."

Her warmth, both of body and of spirit, seduced him. He couldn't think straight with barely a paper width of space separating them. And then there was no space at all when she slid against him, tilting her face toward his expectantly. Her eyes were clear of the doubt and fear he'd seen clouding them so many times in the past days.

Unable to resist her invitation, Dominic met it with one of his own. As their lips met, he silently bade her to love him. As impossible as such a mating seemed to him, he couldn't help wanting what he shouldn't ask for, wanting it with all his heart, soul and every fiber of his being.

Dominic crushed Asia to him, wondering how he would ever let her go.

THE BARE BULB in the shanty glowed dimly through the grimy windows. A silhouette broke in two for a moment, then merged back into a single unit.

The man watching smiled.

"Take your pleasures while you can," he grunted in a low voice.

It wouldn't be long now. The element of surprise shifted the odds in his favor. They would think they were safe, wouldn't be expecting him. He'd have them both where he wanted them. He hadn't forgotten his orders—to kill the woman and anyone else standing in his way. Doing so would be almost as much pleasure as the game they'd been playing. All that was lacking now was opportunity. A patient man when he had to be, he settled back to wait.

Opportunity came less than an hour later. The would-be lovers had been talking most of that time. What a waste. The man was a fool to pass her up while he could have her.

The man came to the window to gaze upon the tracks. He motioned to Asia and she joined him. They seemed to be talking something over, making some decision. Then they moved away together. The room went dark. A moment later, two figures slid from the shanty and over the tracks, dodging around another train being made up. They were headed for the one at the far end of the yard.

He followed, grinning when he caught the number "13" glowing on the switch box. How appropriate. He wondered if they were superstitious. If he was successful, this would be their unlucky night.

Others moved around the yard, as well. Switchmen making up trains. Road crews walking up and down the side of one that was already coupled, first connecting, then checking the air lines. And a few other hoboes busy avoiding the yard bull as they sneaked around and found their hidey-holes.

Pulling a hat low over his forehead, he shifted his backpack, ready to blend in to their midst.

Chapter Eleven

"Empty," Dominic said, flashing a light around the interior of a boxcar. He threw in his duffel bag. "Give me your things."

Asia slipped both bags off her shoulder and handed them over. They quickly joined his.

"Want me to give you a hand?"

His tone was deep and sexy, shooting a thrill down to her toes. Asia wouldn't soon forget the embraces they'd shared. Dominic had done no more than kiss her and carefully explore her body as if gauging her tolerance to him. She'd been surprised—and delighted—that he'd been able to overcome her initial reaction to his touch. She'd stiffened only for a moment. Then, softening under his gentle ministrations and reminding herself that this was Dominic, a man who wouldn't hurt her, she'd relaxed.

Because she'd been afraid she might never want to feel a man's hands on her again, she was high enough on the memory to tease him. "Depends on where you put the hand."

"Anywhere you'd like."

Dominic circled her closely, brushed the side of her neck with his beard-stubbled cheek before giving her the boost. Heat raced through Asia as she clambered onto the boxcar floor, the imprint of his warm fingers on her bottom. She couldn't help thinking about the following hours they would share alone when he rolled up beside her.

"Let's set up for the night at the head of the car," Dominic suggested, getting to his feet and carrying their things forward.

Asia followed, happier than she'd ever thought she could be under the circumstances.

There within the glow of the flashlight, they made up an impromptu seating and sleeping area from discarded sheets of cardboard and from what Dominic called "500-mile paper." He claimed arranging themselves feet forward was safest since cars would probably be switched around more than once on their journey.

"I wouldn't want to see your pretty neck broken from the jolt when a car is switched onto the line," he explained.

For the next hour, they snuggled together and talked quietly about things having nothing to do with their fathers, her attacker or the suspects. They explored each other's personal likes and dislikes. Only once were they interrupted by more than the slam and resounding jolt of car upon car. A pair of hoboes mistakenly thought their boxcar was empty and were about to take possession. Then the two men saw the couple, apologized profusely and went on to find some other hidey-hole.

Finally the train quieted and settled down. She and Dominic continued talking, but he kept checking his watch.

"I haven't heard the engine, yet. I think I'll go see what's taking so long."

She rose with him. "I'll go with you."

"Someone has to stay with our things or they might disappear."

"All right," she agreed.

But she didn't have to like it.

Asia followed him to the open doors and sat at the edge, legs dangling over the side. Across the yard, a hotshot careened northbound without slowing. By the time the caboose had disappeared, so had Dominic.

The night was dark, moonless, chilly.

Asia rubbed her arms and willed him to hurry. Waiting made her impatient. He seemed to be taking forever, and she was getting stiff from the wind that had risen since they'd taken shelter. She hopped down to the ground to stretch her legs and to move around to get her blood flowing but had taken only a few steps before hearing voices nearby.

"We're behind schedule," one grunted as the sound of an engine was followed by a collision and a sharp jerk of the train.

"So start connecting the air line."

As the road crew approached, Asia realized she might not have enough time to get into the car before they spotted her. Instead she fled to the shadow of a lone bulk loader on the next track where she hid from view.

The men passed.

About to return, planning to scramble into the boxcar herself, Asia paused when she thought she heard her name over the din of connecting cars several tracks down. Though she listened intently, she wasn't sure.

She only wished Dominic hadn't left her side. Where in the world was he?

"Asia."

Now certain the whisper was no figment of her imagination, she softly called, "Dom?"

"Over here."

The continuous *clackety-clack* of a slow freight pulling through the station covered anything more he might have said. Cautiously she looked around before wandering out from the shadows.

"Asia, this way, quickly!"

The low command seemed to come from several tracks over, where a string of cars stood in procession. She could barely make out their silhouettes against the faint yard light. Must be another train being made up.

Had Dominic discovered he'd made a mistake, that they'd boarded the wrong freight?

"Dominic, where are you?" she called against the wind.

"Here!" came the impatient answer.

Checking once more to make sure the coast was clear, Asia then sped across the tracks as quickly as possible. By the time she launched herself into the shadows of the train being made up on track eight, she was breathing hard and her heart was pumping like mad. Her adrenaline was on overload.

"Dom?" she called out yet again.

When there was no answer, gooseflesh covered her arms. For the first time, it occurred to her that she might have made a mistake in leaving the safety of the boxcar. Even while logic told her no one could possibly know where they were, instinct countered she could be wrong.

Nerves fluttering through her taut body, she stood still and indecisive.

The continued clack of wheels on rails got to her, made her want to cover her ears. Her heart was pounding in her throat as she stood immobilized trying to make up her mind. What to do? A metallic crack alerted her to another presence, but before she could turn to see the source of the noise, a gross weight fell on her from the car directly behind.

With a yelp, she flew forward, hands out to break her fall across the next set of tracks. Pain fired both palms as they scraped jagged stone, and competed with the agony of her rib cage and shin hitting the steel rails. The air whooshed from her lungs. Even so, frantic to get away from her attacker, she tried to rise, only to be stunned by a vicious cuff to the side of her neck.

She sprawled across the tracks, for the moment unable to move.

Vibration against the side of her face and an ominous *clackety-clack* warned her of oncoming danger.

Groaning, she lifted her head to see a dark bulk closing in on her fast. A loose car! Gathering every vestige of strength she could muster, Asia squirmed and pulled her knees to her chest. She rolled over the rail and onto the sharp stones, flattening herself facedown just as the noise grew to sinister proportions. The car slowed and stopped, its rear wheels mere inches from her body, part of its bulk directly over her head.

"Oh, my God," she muttered, inching herself away from the tracks.

"Asia!"

Panicked when she heard the man's voice calling her name, she scrambled to her knees, then somehow made it up to her feet. She swayed as a numbing pain shot through her when she tried to take a step. Her leg. Dear God, her leg didn't want to hold her!

"Asia, are you all right?"

The voice ahead countered by a scrabbling noise behind confused her. She whirled as a human shadow melded with that of the train car.

"Asia," Dominic said as he came up behind her, making her turn full circle.

"Dominic? Thank God it's you this time. He's here—the man who attacked me. He threw me in front of an oncoming car and then disappeared over there somewhere." Stopping to gulp some air, she indicated the direction. "No matter what we do, he'll find us."

Cursing roundly, Dominic was already jogging away from her. "I'm going after the bastard!"

"No, wait!"

But her cry went unheeded. Asia stared after him, her fear renewing itself, this time for Dominic as he disappeared into the night, possibly to become the next victim.

DOMINIC BARELY caught sight of a figure moving down the length of the train being made up on track eight, but he was after his chimera like a shot, running stealthily and hugging the shadows so he wouldn't be spotted until it was too late for the man to escape. Adrenaline had him pumped, ready for anything.

The distance between them narrowed. Dominic put on speed. A mistake. Loose rock skidded beneath his foot, telegraphing an unmistakable warning.

The man he pursued turned for a second. Dominic could only make out a dark silhouette topped by a brimmed hat before the figure slid between two cars. Dominic slowed, approached the opening cautiously lest this be a trap. But the man had already broached the dangerous coupling and was now running across the next set of tracks.

"You're not getting away this time," Dominic muttered under his breath, "not when I'm so close!"

Grabbing on to the car to his right for safety, he hopped over the coupling as a car switched into place and slammed the rear of the string. The whole line jerked into motion, pitching Dominic toward wheels able to sever a man in half. Holding on for dear life, he hit the metal housing with the flat of his free hand, pushed off and rolled onto the gravel and out of the way. A close call.

Heart pounding, cursing when he realized the other man had gained some distance, he got to his feet and continued the chase with increased determination, only to be stopped cold by a high-pitched whistle and an intense beam piercing the black night. He backed up a few steps as a single engine roared down the track, washing him with its deadly breath.

He set off again as soon as the engine had cleared him.

Up ahead, the other man made the mistake of looking back in Dominic's direction. His foot caught on a rail, sending him off balance. He righted himself but his hat cocked to the side. The wind lifted and spun it away like a feather. Rather than trying to retrieve it, he picked up speed and disappeared behind the control tower.

Already after him, Dominic scooped up the hat on the way and was somewhat disappointed to find it was made of felt rather than straw as he'd assumed. He dropped the thing and continued on to the control tower. To his frustration, he found himself alone. Certain the attacker wouldn't have wandered into the one place he would have been arrested for trespassing, Dominic continued to search the dimly lighted grounds to no avail.

Another engine whistle came from the other side of the yard, alerting him to a different kind of danger. If he didn't get back to Asia pronto, their train was going to take off without them!

He turned to go, raking the surrounding area one last time. Movement caught his gaze. A figure stepped through the light from the dispatch office window. Though he only got a glimpse of the man who crossed it, a glimpse was enough.

This could be no coincidence.

At least now he knew the face of their enemy!

Another blast of the whistle shot his legs with speed as he cut back across the tracks and made for the train whose brakes were being released. Exhaustion was catching up with him in limbs that didn't want to cooperate. He noted Asia was moving even more laboriously toward the freight, glancing over her shoulder as he drew near.

"You made it." She sounded relieved.

"C'mon," he said, grabbing her hand.

"I can't go faster. My leg."

But they had no time to take things slow and easy. The train was starting to pull out of the yard. Dominic hooked her arm over his shoulder and half carried her toward the open maw of the boxcar.

The train was even now picking up speed.

"Use both hands," he shouted over the noise. "Throw your good leg up and roll in and out of my way."

No sooner had he completed his instructions than he was helping her follow them. She flattened her hands against the flooring, threw a leg over the edge, but had trouble on the roll when her other leg contacted metal. She cried out and tried again, this time succeeding with an extra boost from him. But the train was moving even faster before she rolled out of the way.

Dominic's feet slapped numb against the gravel, his legs and lungs pumping hard to keep up. Hauling himself up would take his last ounce of strength. He prayed he wouldn't miss.

"Hurry, Dominic, hurry," Asia shouted.

Hands flat against the metal, he heaved his body upward, found a hold with his inside leg. The train lurched to the side as it rounded a bend, and for a brief moment, he lost his balance. With a supreme effort, he held on for the few seconds it took for the boxcar to steady. Then he lunged forward and rolled. Energy exhausted, he lay there, chest heaving, muscles screaming with the effort.

"You made it," Asia cried. And then, when he didn't respond, asked, "He didn't hurt you, too?"

"No. Give me . . . a minute . . . to catch my breath."

Having stayed in top shape due to the physical labor he'd been doing over the past two years, Dominic recovered quickly. He found his flashlight and shone it over Asia. She was covered with filth, and her hands looked raw as she gingerly rubbed her left shin.

"Talk about bruises—I can't wait to see this one," she said, her pain apparent in her voice.

"I'll take a look. Think you can make it to the head of the car?"

She nodded and, with his support, moved in that direction. Her limp seemed less pronounced than it had been when she was running to the train.

"I'm getting the feeling in my leg back," she said in explanation, following that with a good-natured complaint. "But I'm not liking it."

A moment later they were seated on their make-shift bed. Dominic was glad to note their bags were still intact if for no other reason than to find some way to relieve Asia's pain.

"Can you pull up the leg of your jeans?" he asked.

Asia complied. The denim clung to her calf, the narrow leg barely going high enough to reveal the injury. The beam of his flashlight easily picked out the swollen discolored area, the center of which was a bright, angry red.

"You need an ice pack on that."

"Let's have room service send one up," she joked.

He ran his hands over her leg, starting at the ankle and gently working his way up. It was only with difficulty that he distracted himself from any thoughts but checking her out for a fracture. He wanted to take her in his arms, kiss away all her hurts, make love to her until neither of them could think of anything but each other. Instead he remained clinical, almost detached. He was proud of his control.

When he touched her near the bruised swelling, however, her sharp intake of breath and automatic recoil went straight to his heart.

"Sorry. I guess you can feel everything just fine. You'll be glad to know there doesn't seem to be a break." Pulling his shaving kit from his duffel bag, he found two extra-strength aspirin and a hip flask of water. "Take these."

He then removed a small bottle of antiseptic and some gauze pads.

When she was finished with the water, he cleaned off her scraped palms, which had looked worse than they actually were because some blood had mixed with the dirt. Beneath the grime, she had a few scratches and a couple of raw spots, but no deep cuts or punctures. She barely winced when he applied the antiseptic.

"I have an idea for your leg that might sound silly."

"Anything that'll help."

He dug deep into his duffel and came up with two cans of soda that had been kept insulated by his clothing and were therefore still cold.

"Not ice, but they'll do," he said, showing her. "I'll need your scarf."

Asia snorted but untied the bedraggled piece of cloth from around her neck. "Here you go, Doc."

"This may smart." Even though he carefully set the cans over the bruised and swollen area, he was unable to miss her grimace. "You hold the cans in place while I secure them."

"Did anyone ever tell you that you have a bizarre mind?" she asked as she placed her hands over his.

"Inventive," he countered.

Dominic was relieved that Asia could make jokes. That meant she wasn't in such bad shape, after all. Slipping his hands free, he looped the scarf around the cans and made a knot that would be easy to undo. Then he drew back and admired his handiwork.

"You could start a new trend."

Asia held out her leg and studied it. "Hmm. Not exactly what I would call fashionable. But it is ingenious," she admitted. "And as long as I don't have to do any walking, this should work."

Dominic checked his watch. "We'll give it twenty minutes, then remove the cans. You should have ice on that part of your leg every hour. Unfortunately I didn't buy more, so I'll have to get my hands on some of the real stuff later."

What he really wanted to get his hands on was Asia herself, but he was afraid meeting her attacker had been too much for her to cope with. If she had been willing earlier, she might reject him now. He clicked off the flashlight to conserve the batteries and tortured himself by sitting close to her, shoulder to shoulder, thigh to thigh.

When she settled in, he said, "I know who your attacker is now."

"Why didn't you say so? You caught up to him?"

"No, I lost the man, but just before coming back to the train, I spotted him near the dispatch office. He walked right through a lighted area. It was George Yerkes."

"You're certain?"

"Positive. Not that I can prove he's the one who tried to kill you if it came to a court of law. We don't exactly have evidence." Dominic mentally castigated himself. "I knew the guy looked familiar. I must have seen him with my father at some time. Things should have clicked before, especially after I got a look at that tattoo.''

''You didn't tell me about any tattoo.''

''I saw it at the lumber camp, but I couldn't figure out why I felt like I should be able to place it. Now I remember. When I was a kid, my father had a letter opener of the same design on his desk. A dagger with a snake wrapped around the handle. And his accountant had a key chain with the same insignia. I think my father used it as identification for members of his organization. A king cobra, one of the most poisonous snakes in the world. Fitting, huh?''

He stopped when he realized that Asia had stiffened beside him.

''The flashlight,'' she said, ''where is it?''

Dominic found the light on the floor and gave it to her. ''What's wrong.''

She flicked on the beam and searched through her overnight bag from which she pulled her toiletries kit.

''I don't believe it. At first I didn't tell you about this because I didn't know whether or not to trust you. Then I just plain forgot.''

From a pocket on the side of the soft bag, she withdrew something long and shiny—a gold chain, hanging from which was a gold medallion. She held the piece steady under the flashlight beam. Imprinted on the metal was a dagger with a snake wrapped around the shaft.

A king cobra.

Dominic took the medallion from her. ''This design is identical to the tattoo. Where did you get it?''

''From the man who attacked me.''

Elation swept through him. "We've got it, then—the physical evidence we need to nail the bastard! Proof that George Yerkes has been trying to kill you!"

ASIA LAY IN THE DARK pressed against Dominic's chest and trying to sleep, long after their discovery. She couldn't relax, couldn't let her mind drift. Exhaustion should have sucked her into sleep's arms long ago, but she was wired. There was too much happening, and too many things to think about.

Especially Dominic. What would happen once they found Jessica?

Would he be willing to stick around, make a new life with her? One that would maximize his potential. Or would he sneak away to hide working on a ferryboat or for a logging company or doing some other job that he didn't care about?

The thought of not ever seeing him again frightened her almost as much as the possibility of seeing Yerkes.

She turned restlessly in Dominic's arms, trying to get closer to his warmth.

Immediately he asked, "The leg bothering you?"

"A little."

They'd taken the soda cans off long ago. The cold added to the aspirin had helped. Sharp pain had receded but was now a low if tolerable throbbing.

"Anything I can do to make you more comfortable?"

"Just hold me," she said, wanting so much more.

Dominic pulled her closer, wrapped his other arm around her so he had her cocooned. She fought the suffocating feeling that tried to intrude, and reciprocated by placing a scraped palm on Dominic's chest.

His heart beat strongly... too strongly for him to fall asleep. He was as aware of her as she was of him, but he wasn't doing anything about it.

Certain the first move would have to be up to her, she slid her hand beneath the plaid flannel and traced his collarbone through the thin material of his T-shirt.

"Asia..."

"Shh."

She didn't want him to stop her exploration as she became familiar with the strong cords of his neck. The pulse in his throat beat against her fingers. Then his beard stubble assaulted her, the tiny pinpricks making her tender palm throb with life. He cupped her hand with his, nuzzled and kissed the scraped flesh... then tried to remove her hand to some safer place.

Safer for him, Asia thought.

"Don't," she pleaded.

The struggle was short-lived. Dominic groaned and shifted, his warm breath fanning her face as he explored in the dark, somehow unerringly finding her mouth.

He was tender.

Too tender.

Asia demanded his strength. Threading her fingers through his short hair, she crushed herself against him and deepened the kiss.

He tried to pull away.

She went with him, rolling on top of him, mentally blocking out the throbbing in her leg. That she was hurting physically was of no consequence. More important, her emotions were on edge. She was afraid that if she didn't press the issue, she might never know what it would be like to share herself with the man she loved.

For she did love Dominic. She knew that now.

Ridiculous that such an important event in a person's life could happen so fast, without fanfare, without warning. Ridiculous that it could take her by such surprise. She'd had no choice in the matter, had not been polled. She was stuck with the feeling.

Not that she wanted to deny it or herself.

Asia was grateful that something so special had happened to her in the midst of mayhem. Perhaps this was fate's way of making it up to her, countering the fears her attacker had conjured when he'd tried to rape her. She would never forget that night—it was burned into her memory—but she could depersonalize the event.

The man she loved could neutralize the imprint of those hands that had hurt her.

Dominic's hands were roaming her now. Her back, sides, waist, hips. Wanting more intimacy, she shifted restlessly, felt his immediate and very male response. She flushed with need, hurt with arousal and was certain he felt the same. Catching Dominic by the wrist, Asia pulled his hand around and trapped it between their bodies, leaving him with no doubts as to what she desired.

"Asia, do you know what you're doing?"

Knowing exactly what she wanted, she kissed him passionately.

"If you want to stop," he warned her, "do it now."

In answer, she found his throat with her lips. Her tongue explored the sweat-stained, salty skin there. Her teeth nipped the flesh between neck and shoulder.

Dominic shuddered, and to her gratitude, stopped trying to fight what they both wanted. Before she knew what was happening, he took control of the situation. He unsnapped and unzipped her jeans and delved beneath her briefs.

The train was a living thing beneath them, around them. It enveloped them in movement and sound whose harmony was difficult to resist.

Dominic released her so they could quickly open or remove enough clothing to come together.

Without further preliminaries, Asia found and guided him to her. Dominic didn't hesitate, but impaled her with an urgency she matched. He filled her, made her complete. For the moment, nothing but this mating mattered. Asia gave in to sensation, spurred him to drive deeper and harder. She felt as if he could pierce her straight to her very soul.

As they moved, one to the other, she focused on the train's rhythm, absorbed the clacking of wheels on rails. For a few moments, they were an integral part of the train, speeding toward a crucial destination.

Only afterward, when they lay tangled together, did reality send its chilly fingers up her spine.

What if this really was the only time she and Dominic would have together? The thought drove her to desperation, to declare herself and force a declaration from him if she could.

"I love you," she whispered, disappointed by the silence that followed.

If he couldn't say the words, Dominic wrapped her closer to his chest, made her feel safe for the moment.

But what of tomorrow?

"What's going to happen once we find Jessica?" she asked.

"I'm going to bring her to see our father. He'll end the vendetta and everyone will live happily ever after."

"Will they?" Asia knew she shouldn't press him but couldn't help herself. "What about you? What will you do?"

"Stick around for as long as Jess needs me, I guess. Finding a job shouldn't be difficult. I can do anything that takes some muscle."

"What about something more challenging?"

What about me? she wanted to ask.

Dominic avoided answering by carefully setting her aside and gathering together the clothing they'd scattered.

"Better get dressed," he said gruffly. "You never know when we might pull into a station."

Asia bit back her frustration and tried to tell herself she was content.

A lie.

Whether Dominic stayed in Seattle to protect his sister or went elsewhere to get another job that would be meaningless to him, the end result would be the same.

Either way, she was bound to lose him.

Chapter Twelve

The freight pulled into Portland in the small hours of the morning while darkness still cloaked the city. Jumping out of the boxcar first, Dominic helped Asia down and held her longer than was necessary.

This time *she* pulled away.

And well he deserved such cool treatment, idiot that he was. He'd had the perfect opportunity to tell her he loved her, to ask her to give him time to work things out, time to get his life back together. The little voice inside his head chanted "Oil and water don't mix" preventing him from giving way to emotion.

And now he'd almost convinced himself they were both better off being allies rather than lovers. *She'd* be better off, at any rate.

"Control tower is over there," Asia said. Her voice was nearly as severe as her expression. "I guess we'd better head that way."

About to agree, Dominic was distracted for a moment when he noticed movement farther along the line of cars. A man slid down the ladder of a reefer. From this distance, Dominic couldn't see much, couldn't tell whether or not the freight hopper could possibly be Yerkes.

He was looking for monsters in the shadows, Dominic told himself. Perhaps the villain had no idea of where they'd been headed. Perhaps Yerkes had been scared off. Then, again, perhaps he was trying too hard to be positive. Yerkes had found them before—he could do it again.

The question was not "whether" but "how soon."

"Well, *I'm* going," Asia muttered to herself.

She reached past him to grab her bags from the metal floor. And then she was off, her limp barely noticeable now, though Dominic had never found ice to get the swelling down. Swinging his duffel bag over his right shoulder, he caught up to Asia easily and wrested the overnight bag from her grasp.

"Better balance if there's an even load," he said, and before she could object, swung it over the left shoulder.

Asia didn't argue. She pursed her lips and didn't say a word as they crossed the tracks while carefully staying out of harm's way. Her sullen silence made Dominic uneasy. She could be a firecracker when she chose. She'd raked him over the coals when she'd wanted his help. Her unusual disposition proved to him how deeply he'd hurt her.

Switching-yard activity was slower than it had been in Tacoma, and so Dominic was a bit off guard. He didn't see the yard worker until they were caught in the brilliant beam of a large light.

"Can I help you folks?" the deep-voiced man barked.

"We were wondering when a train might be going out to Klamoth Bend," Dominic said, keeping his voice even and slightly deferential. Honey worked better than vinegar on these guys. "Sure would appreciate it if you could tell us."

The worker looked them over for an uncomfortable moment, making Dominic wonder if they were going to get kicked out of the yard this time.

Then the man grunted, "They're making up your train now over on track ten. You'd best get over there soon."

Flashing his beam at the ground, the man started to walk on. Before he could escape, however, Asia asked, "When did the last freight go out to Klamoth Bend?"

"Same time yesterday morning," the man called over his shoulder without breaking stride.

"Thanks." She turned to Dominic, speaking to him with more ease than she had in hours. "Do you realize what that means? That Peggy Shield couldn't have left for Klamoth Bend yet. She might be somewhere here in this yard. Let's get over to track ten."

They doubled back, found the train and began searching the cars. The first few were empty of people, but a scrawny bearded man was curled into a ball in the cubbyhole of a bulk loader.

"Hey, pal," Dominic said in a soft voice. "You seen many other hoppers on this freight?"

"A few."

"What about a woman?" Drawing on their tall tale yet again, he said, "We're looking for my wife's sister."

"There's a dame traveling with a coupla men. I saw 'em get in the next box."

But that proved to be a dud. The woman was around forty, too old to be Peggy Shield. And none of the three people had seen another woman, alone or otherwise.

Activity at the front of the train drew Dominic's attention. The road crew was approaching. He realized they weren't going to finish searching all the cars before the freight took off. They'd have to finish the job at the first stop. In the meantime, he didn't want Asia running to board another boxcar as it picked up speed.

He spotted a caboose in transit, positioned a few dozen cars forward of the working caboose at the end of the train. That meant it should be empty since it was merely being transported to another yard. Most freight hoppers would avoid the increased possibility of getting kicked off by boarding one, but Dominic was willing to take the chance for Asia's sake.

"We'd better split up," Dominic told her. He pointed. "Why don't you check the boxcar before the caboose in the middle of the line. Then wait for me outside. I'll join you as soon as I check out the others."

Looking around nervously, she said, "Don't be too long, okay?"

"I'll stay within yelling distance."

That is, if she had the chance to yell should she run into Yerkes....

Asia was already walking away, her gait uneven. Dominic thought to stop her but held himself in check. She wouldn't appreciate his treating her like a child. Besides, she would be fine on her own for a few minutes.

He wouldn't be far away.

Even so, Dominic determined to hurry lest some dreadful new "accident" befall the woman he loved.

AFTER WHAT HAD HAPPENED to her in Tacoma, Asia wasn't entirely comfortable leaving Dominic, even if only for a few minutes. But she realized they didn't have much time. She didn't want to hold him back. He could search more rapidly without her limping along beside him.

The boxcar he'd asked her to check was empty of passengers as far as she could tell. Lumber filled the interior. Only a few feet of space was left between the top of the piles and the roof of the car.

Glancing back down the line, she noted Dominic had already checked several cars and was climbing up the side of another on a metal ladder. He had a few more cars to go and wouldn't be long in joining her. Standing around talking near the engine, the road crew looked as if they were ready to start connecting the air line.

She moved toward the caboose. The sky had lightened from black to a deep blue gray. Almost dawn. Though she wore a thin long-sleeved sweatshirt that she'd dug out of her bag, she was chilled not so much from the cold as from being alone.

And afraid.

Fear took many faces as she was swiftly learning. There was physical and psychological fear as inspired by Yerkes and his special brand of brutality. But then there was the emotional fear that Dominic wanted nothing more of her than what she'd earlier offered— no, to be truthful, what she'd forced on him.

And it was the very strident sound of live fear she heard coming from the interior of the caboose.

"No, don't!"

A woman's voice, followed by a man's. Asia couldn't make out what he was saying, but she recognized the threatening tone. Her flesh crawled as she stood frozen, listening. A woman's moan. Sounds of a struggle. A crash followed by a feminine wail.

"Help, some—"

The rest was garbled as if her mouth were being covered by a hand.

Before Asia knew what she was about, she flew around toward the caboose. Her heart hammered at her chest, her pulse at her jugular. She was familiar with that particular sound of fear, had voiced it herself only nights before.

The woman was being assaulted, and Asia couldn't stand outside and pretend it wasn't happening.

Climbing the metal steps in seconds, she turned the handle of the door and threw the panel open so hard its window vibrated ominously. Entering, she squinted against the dim light, was barely able to make out two forms struggling at the other end of the sparsely furnished room.

A man pressing a struggling, desperate woman onto a cot. One hand was on her throat, the other roaming her body.

Asia's gorge rose at the sight. Grabbing her shoulder bag by its strap and screaming, she flew at the man without concern for her own safety.

"Get off her!" The weight of the heavy purse came down full force on the back of his head. "Leave her be!"

"Hey, what the—"

"Get out of here before I kill you!"

At that moment, Asia meant what she said. She saw red. She remembered how it felt to be a victim. She remembered feeling helpless, thinking she was powerless.

Well, she wasn't powerless now.

The man whipped around as the bag came down once more, this time bashing him square in the face. The other woman rallied and shoved him with all her strength. He flew off the cot and down to his knees on the floor.

Asia continued to use her purse as a weapon, but she wasn't the only one hitting him. In silent fury, the other woman was pummeling him with both fists. He was frantically trying to cover his head and face, trying to protect himself by using his arms as shields.

"You scum!" the other woman screamed in a shrill voice. "Men like you should be castrated!"

At that the man capitulated. "I'm outta here!" He nearly knocked Asia over as he made for the door and slammed it behind him as if he were afraid they would follow.

The woman who'd been attacked jumped up from the cot. She was panting, and wiping the tears from her face with her shirtsleeve.

"Oh, God, if you hadn't come along, he would have—"

"I know." Swallowing hard, Asia wrapped comforting arms around the slight figure and patted her thin back. "But you're all right now."

"I thought I was safe in here. I'm usually so careful. How can I thank you?"

"That's not necessary."

Asia sat heavily in a chair, even as she took a better look at the intended victim. Mid-twenties, medium height, on the thin side... she'd memorized the description and this woman fitted it perfectly.

"You can travel with my friend and me." And even though Asia was certain she knew the answer, she asked, "How far are you going?"

"Klamoth Bend." The woman took something from her pack on the floor. A click and a soft glow lighted the immediate area. She set the battery-powered lantern on a decrepit table. "My name's Peggy. Peggy Shield."

Asia's heart began to thunder. So she'd done it. She'd finally caught up with the elusive woman! Thanking the heavens, she stared at strands of light brown hair that escaped a knit cap and hung around a pretty, oddly familiar face.

"Peggy Shield," she echoed, wondering how to approach the woman about Dominic's sister, wondering why she was getting this strange, unsettling feeling about the matter. She'd had enough of games. Direct was best. "Aren't you friends with a woman named Jessica?"

Peggy tensed and her eyes went wide. In the light of the lantern, they looked green rather than the hazel reported in the Mountain Timber employee records.

Before Asia knew it, the woman bolted for the door.

"Wait a minute!" Asia protested, flying to her feet and going after her. "You can't leave!" She grabbed the woman's arm.

"Let me go!"

"I've got to talk to you." Asia's mind was spinning. Where was Dominic? "It's important."

"No!"

They struggled, Asia merely trying to hang on to the woman for whom they'd spent so much time searching—and who now was doing her very best to get away once more. Asia ducked a set of nails that went for her face.

A metallic click signaled the door's reopening and made both women freeze.

Had the attacker returned, perhaps with reinforcements?

"Asia?" came Dominic's voice, followed by his large body blocking the doorway.

Sighing in relief, Asia released her bulldog grip on the other woman who'd gone still as death. Her delicate face was turned toward the door, her mouth open. Then Dominic took a good look at the smaller woman in return and his eyes went wide.

"Jess?" he asked, sounding awed. "Is it really you?"

"Dominic?" Then louder and happier, "Dom!"

Jessica Crawley launched herself at her brother whose arms snaked around her thin back. He lifted her, laughing.

"Jess, oh, Jess. We found you." He twirled her around and moved her farther into the car where he set her down but didn't let go. "I'm sorry," he whispered, sounding choked. "I'm sorry I wasn't there for you when you needed me."

Asia's eyelids stung as she watched the tearful reunion. She backed away from brother and sister and drew closer to the door. Meaning to give them some privacy, she couldn't stop herself from listening as she stared out into the semidark.

"I missed you so much," Dominic was saying. "I'll never forgive myself for giving up on you, for not looking for you sooner." He laughed. "We've been searching for a woman named Peggy Shield and found you instead."

"We're one and the same," Jessica admitted. "Since I wanted to disappear, I wasn't about to use my real name. How did you find me?"

Dominic brought her up to date, starting with the visit to their mother and ending with an introduction to Asia.

"Marcie called and told me some woman named Asia was claiming to be my sister," Jessica admitted. "Had she mentioned Dominic, I might have stuck around Mountain Timber. I suspected someone might be looking for 'Peggy' to get to me, so I doctored the employee records by adding a file for 'Jessica.'" Her smile faded and she looked puzzled. "Why did you come looking for me now?"

"To bring you home."

"No! I can't go back."

"Jess, I'll be there for you this time," Dominic said. "You don't have to worry about the bastard who raped you anymore. I heard he met with a fatal accident."

"Daddy," Jessica whispered knowingly. She shook her head. "This once I can't say I'm sorry." She sounded truly frightened when she said, "But Daddy has other enemies—"

"I'll stick around as long as you need me," Dominic interrupted, pulling off the knit cap. "You changed your hair color.'' His emotions clear on his face, he gently touched a strand. ''And you've lost so much weight.''

Asia mentally backed off from the tender scene. She should be happy. They'd found the one person who could get to King Crawley. And Dominic was reunited with his sister, would be with his family. No matter that Jessica was still protesting. Dominic would convince her.

Not wanting either of them to see the tears welling in her eyes, Asia left the caboose, rushed down the steps, then moved away from the train as she realized the road crew was getting closer, connecting the air line.

What was wrong with her? Instead of crying, she should be rejoicing. But any celebration would be halfhearted, Asia thought.

For she'd already lost Dominic, just as she'd known she would.

JASPER RAFERTY LAY in his bed in the cardiac intensive care unit, lost in his own guilt. He didn't believe he would make it out of the sterile place, but perhaps that would be best for everyone. He might as well face facts—his life was over in any event. He'd lost everything he'd cared about when he'd betrayed his ethics.

His brush with death had clarified a lot of things for him.

He was a failure both as a judge and as a parent. He couldn't protect those he loved no matter how much he wished it, no matter how hard he tried.

The feeling of impotency threatened to smother him.

Better that he die than see even one of his children go to the grave before him, knowing *he* was the reason.

He lay with his eyes closed, searching for a way to end all this misery. Perhaps if he pulled the life-giving oxygen tube from his nose...

They would merely replace the tube—maybe even tie his hands down so he couldn't do so again—and he would be a failure yet again.

"Father?" The edge of the bed bowed and a hand lifted his while another covered it. "Father, the doctors say you're not fighting hard enough to get well. You have to try. Please. We need you."

Jasper wondered if he were hallucinating. Dakota's voice, not harsh and judgmental, but filled with sorrow. Pleading. His son calling him "Father" again, wanting him to live.

"I need you. I didn't mean some of the things I said to you. I... I love you."

Forcing open his eyes, Jasper focused on the handsome, virile man who was his son. Dakota's worried expression eased a bit. Jasper opened his mouth, groped for his voice.

"Shhh, you don't have to say anything now."

"Must... while I can."

"Father, if only you make your best effort, you'll be fine. Once you're home, we'll have plenty of time to talk."

But Jasper feared his son was deluded. This might be the only chance he had. He couldn't pass it up. "Forgive me, Dakota, please."

"I already have." His son squeezed his hand. "I was so angry that I spoke before I had time to think things over. I'm sorry."

Jasper nodded. Elation filled his breast, fluttered his heart alarmingly, triggered an uneven set of beeps on the monitoring equipment they'd hooked him up to.

"Never forget your principles," Jasper croaked, "not for a moment."

"I won't, but if I should be tempted, you'll be around to keep me in line, right?"

A nurse opened the curtain enclosure, which Dakota must have drawn for privacy. She immediately went to Jasper's side, eyes quickly scanning the monitoring equipment.

She spoke to Dakota in a low voice. "I'm sorry, but you'll have to leave. You're exciting your father too much. He needs his rest."

Jasper tried to protest that he didn't want his son to leave, but Dakota had already risen and was backing away from the bed.

"I'll be in to see you later, Father. You do as the nurse says. We want you home where you belong."

As Jasper stared at his son's departing back, he determined to get there. Home . . . what was left of what had once been a well-furnished, nicely tended if modest estate. He would do his best to get well, to seek one last ray of happiness before death claimed him. But he must do something else immediately, must clear his conscience as best he could.

Before the busy nurse could leave, he stopped her. "I need paper and a pen."

"Later, Mr. Raferty. Perhaps after a nap."

"Now!"

The single word uttered with all his strength set the monitors askew once more.

"All right. I'll get them for you if you promise to keep yourself calm."

Jasper nodded and the nurse hurried off to find the writing implements.

Tempted to confess all to the authorities, he hesitated. They might not be able to help Asia or to stop Crawley from playing out his heartless game of revenge. And once the authorities were involved, his children would be wreathed in scandal and ruin.

It was enough that he'd ruined his own life.

The nurse returned and set the paper and pen on a tray she swung over his bed. After using a control that propped up the head end of his mattress, she stood a respectful distance away while he did what he had to.

Difficult. So difficult. His hand trembled as he scratched out the letter of resignation—he could no longer in good conscience remain on the bench.

When he was done, he felt as if a weight had been lifted from his soul. He was giving up the one thing in life that had meant anything to him other than his family, but the act had freed him to get well, had given him something to look forward to. Though Sydney had never verbally passed judgment on him, Dakota had. His resignation should satisfy the son who had finally forgiven him.

Now if only the last of his prayers would be answered... if only Asia survived King Crawley's madness so that he could ask for his youngest child's forgiveness, as well.

HAVING AVOIDED RUNNING into the road crew by circling several cars lined up on the next track, Asia didn't leave her hiding place until the men disappeared. She couldn't believe that Dominic had not yet succeeded in getting his sister off the train so they could get on with ending the vendetta.

And then an ill-favored thought struck her: what if Jessica refused to intercede with their father on her family's behalf?

The last few days would have been for nothing. All the anxiety. All the danger. And Jessica's refusal would spell the end for her and Dakota and Sydney unless they went underground until Crawley died. Even then, they might never be safe. Loyalties among organization members were legendary.

A noisy hiss heralded the release of pressure on the brakes. The engine blasted a warning. The freight was ready to leave the yard.

Asia flew across the open space between the tracks, intending to make her way to the caboose, to hurry Dominic and his sister. But as she passed a fuel tanker, she had the distinct feeling she wasn't alone. She glanced over her shoulder to see a human form silhouetted against the still-dark blue gray sky. The impression lasted only a second before the figure disappeared several car lengths behind.

Heart thudding, Asia told herself she was jumping to conclusions, that undoubtedly the other person was merely another hobo in transit. She almost had herself convinced until she looked behind her a second time and realized the shadowy figure was closing the gap between them. Her mouth went dry as she realized the implications of leading him directly to the caboose! Dominic was there. And Jessica. Weaponless. They could make sitting ducks for a clever murderer.

Ahead, several cars in front of the caboose, heavy machinery had been loaded onto a flatcar. The engine blasted again. Heart in her throat, Asia said a quick prayer and struggled over the coupling between the tanker and a piggyback. Thankfully the freight didn't start up while she was doing so. When her feet touched the ground on the other side, she released her indrawn breath and hoped she could lose her pursuer long enough to hide. She would try to fool the villain into believing she wasn't on the train at all.

She rapidly made for the flatcar, her footsteps muffled by the hissing brakes. The wheels began to grind as they finally screeched to a start. If only the person following her would fall beneath the wheels their troubles would be at a temporary halt!

She slowed to a stop and mentally prepared herself to board, hoping her leg wouldn't hinder her. Adrenaline had made her forget about the injury for a while. As the flatcar crept past, she switched directions and moved with the train. Remembering Dominic's instructions, she heaved herself up, threw her weight and good leg forward, then rolled onto the flooring and away from the edge.

Her legs were shaky as she rose, the bruised shin throbbing. Her breath came shallow as she wildly sought a place to hide.

She didn't get the chance to find cover.

Grabbed from behind, Asia tried to scream, but a hand over her mouth smothered the sound, and strong arms forced her back into the shadows.

"Shhh," came a woman's desperate whisper. "We can hide in here."

The next thing Asia knew, she was being shoved onto the floor of a tractor cab.

And Marijo Lunt dropped directly on top of her.

"JESS, COME ON. We've got to get off this train now!" Dominic yelled.

He pulled his sister onto the platform of the caboose, and although he had hold of her left hand, she stubbornly latched onto the rail with her right. While she had the strength of a madwoman at the moment, Dominic was by far the stronger. But, no matter how desperate he was, he couldn't stand the thought of hurting her through force.

"Dom, you can't make me go back!"

"We'll talk about this in Portland, but now we have to get off and find Asia. I can't leave her alone."

"Then go."

"I can't leave you alone, either!"

No matter that he'd spent the last quarter of an hour explaining every detail of their father's plot against the Rafertys. Jessica was too terrified to agree to anything at this point. Dominic shifted his weight as the car rounded a soft bend and tried again.

"Please, Jess, let's get off while we still can, before the train picks up too much speed."

"You can go, but I'm staying."

"Damn it, Jess!" He let go of his sister and looked over the switching yard in disgust.

Where the hell was Asia? What had prompted her to disappear just when success was within their grasp?

As soon as he talked some sense into his sister, that was.

"Wait a minute, Dom. Look there."

Dominic whipped around and sought the spot Jessica indicated. "What?"

"Someone hopped the flatcar."

"Asia?" Dominic strained to see through the morning's dark skies.

"I don't know. It could have been her, though."

Then the train straightened and the flatcar was out of sight once more. Now Dominic didn't know what to do. If Asia *was* on the train and he managed to get his sister off, he would be abandoning the woman he'd sworn to protect.

He cursed his predicament.

And pushed his sister back into the caboose.

He would have to take the chance of finding Asia at the first stop. In the meantime, he would pray the person Jessica had spotted really had been the woman he loved.

THEY'D BOTH KNOWN the exact second he'd launched himself onto the flatcar—the train had been taking a curve—and Marijo had unnecessarily clamped her hand over Asia's mouth again.

Through the *clackety-clack* of wheels on steel, Asia picked out the sounds of footsteps drawing near. Her heart was beating so loud she swore her pursuer could hear it.

He came closer...and passed by without wavering.

Her breath shuddered through her and she relaxed as much as she could under the circumstances. Above, Marijo did the same, even rolled her weight to one side. The redhead held a hand out to indicate their continued silence.

They waited. And waited. Asia heard nothing askew.

Marijo finally seemed satisfied. With an audible sigh, she leaned back against the gearshift box. Even so, they were cramped together, barely an inch between them.

"Who the hell are you?" Asia asked, her words so soft as to be almost unintelligible.

"Your father sent me to keep you safe, but it's been a hell of a job, let me tell you, Asia Raferty!"

"You're a cop?" The question came out a furious hiss.

Marijo put a finger to her lips and mouthed, "Excon." She listened intently for a moment, then quietly explained. "I owed your father one. I was sent up for robbery with my boyfriend. He was what you might call a bad influence, and I was definitely stupid. I guess your father believed that, because he recommended me for an early release and rehabilitation program. I guess he saw through my tough act."

"And you were supposed to do what?" Asia asked, thoroughly amazed at the unexpected turn of events. "Find me and bring me home?"

"Protect you." Marijo sounded regretful when she said, "I haven't done such a swell job, huh?"

"So that's why you followed me through the woods to the logging site."

"And almost got you killed."

"Yerkes was the one who almost killed me."

"Yerkes?"

Asia recognized the uncertainty in Marijo's voice. "I had my own doubts until Dominic told me about Yerkes's tattoo." She explained the similarity to the medallion. "And last night someone tried to kill me in Tacoma by pushing me in front of a loose freight car. Dominic went after him and spotted Yerkes by the dispatch office."

Marijo seemed to mull that over. "Hmm, I did think it might be him for a while myself, but then I thought...well, never mind."

"You were suspect yourself," Asia informed her.

"Yeah, people have been suspecting me of wrong-doing most of my life. Sometimes they've even been right. My having your comb probably didn't inspire trust. When you let me off in Tacoma, I was ready to tell you everything."

"But I wouldn't listen." Remembering Marijo's expression when they'd left her standing on the street, Asia shifted and tried to find a comfortable position. "Don't you think it's safe to get out of here now? Yerkes probably jumped off when he didn't find me."

"Or he could be searching other cars."

"Other...oh, God, I never thought of that. If he does, he'll find Dominic and Jessica."

"Jessica Crawley?" Marijo's voice rose. "You found her? Then what are you doing on this train? Why aren't you on your way back to Seattle?"

A question Asia wished she herself could answer. "I don't think Dominic convinced her to come back with us. If Yerkes finds them, he might kill them both."

"Maybe we can warn them. What do you think of going from car to car on a moving train?"

Asia's stomach turned over at the thought. "Not much." But if Dominic's life was at stake... "Let's go."

Cramped as she'd been in the small space, Asia was stiff as she half rose and scooted out of Marijo's way. The redhead sat up on her side of the cab, and both women cautiously peered out the windows in every direction. Dawn had finally broken and the gray of early morning was lifting. Try as she might, Asia saw nothing threatening waiting for them except what would undoubtedly be a frightening road ahead.

The freight had left Portland behind and was ascending into the mountains.

"I guess we're clear," Marijo said, opening the door.

She left the cab, Asia following. They made their way around the tractor and some implements lashed to the flatcar. A grapple and heel boom used in logging sat before them, taking up almost the entire width of the flatcar's base.

"How are we going to get around that thing without breaking our necks?" Asia asked.

"Carefully," Marijo answered.

And then another voice, a male voice from behind them asked, "Why even try? Why don't you make things easy for me just this once?"

Heart pumping like mad, Asia turned and came face-to-face with her nemesis. "You!"

His lips lifted into an evil grin as he replied, "Who else, sweetcakes?"

Chapter Thirteen

An openmouthed Asia tried to assimilate the irrefutable: Eddy Voss—not George Yerkes—was the man who'd been trying to kill her.

She shook her head. "I don't understand. What about the tattoo?"

Obviously unfamiliar with Yerkes's anatomy, Eddy frowned. "You don't have to understand nothing except you're gonna die." His head whipped around to Marijo as she moved away from Asia. "Where do you think you're going?"

"To get out of your way," Marijo said, the significant crook of her head indicating Asia should do the same by moving in the opposite direction.

Eddy laughed. "You puny dames really think you can get away from me?"

Asia was wondering the same thing as she eyed the tiny space between the grapple and the outside edge of the car floor. Climbing ever higher, the freight tenaciously clung to the mountainside. A fall off a moving train at any time would undoubtedly result in broken bones. Asia figured a fall here would be fatal.

"Sometimes brains are more important than brawn," Marijo asserted as she continued backing away from Eddy.

"Hey!" He moved toward the redhead threateningly.

"Run, Asia!"

Asia didn't hesitate, but Eddy faltered in confusion long enough for both women to get a head start. Asia hung on to a strip of metal that bit into her palms and, ignoring both the sharp pain and the racing ground below, edged her way around the equipment.

"I hope you're more athletic than I am," Marijo said as she slid toward Asia on the other side. She pointed to the ladder on the following car. "You go first."

"You want me to jump?" Asia's heart lurched as the tracks streaked beneath the coupling.

But Eddy was clinging to the machinery, searching for a foothold on the back edge of the flatcar.

"What did you think we were going to do?" Marijo demanded, pushing her into place. "It won't be as far as it looks. The train is moving to meet you, remember. Don't look down and don't miss! Go!"

Concentrating on the ladder, Asia took a deep breath and leaped just as Eddy caught up to them. He cursed loudly, and she felt his fingers grasp the back of her T-shirt... and tear away.

Then a wall of metal smacked into her, ricocheting pain through her body and stealing her breath away. She grabbed for a rung of the ladder as gravity sucked her downward.

Her fingers connected. She tightened her grip and hung from the metal bar by one hand.

A whoosh of air made her legs bob—her feet were mere inches from the deadly tracks below. Asia tried not to panic, struggled to right herself, to find a foothold. Her wrist was burning and her shoulder felt as if her arm were being pulled from its socket.

"Let go!" Eddy urged with a laugh. "Make my job easier for once!"

"Don't do it!" Marijo shouted. "You can make it. Get to Dominic!"

"Shut up!"

Finding a ledge for her foot just as the other woman screamed in terror, Asia turned to the heartbreaking sound.

Face a horrified mask, Marijo whipped away from the freight, her arms outstretched, hands open, fingers clawing at air. Then, flailing like a rag doll, she picked up speed and plummeted to the slanted ground below.

"Marijo!"

And then Asia could see no more as the train rounded a curve.

Her stomach clenched and threatened to empty. She clutched at the ladder with both hands. Hot tears stung the back of her eyelids for the woman who'd merely been trying to save her life as a favor to her father. If she wasn't quick, she would be next, and Marijo would have fallen to her death for nothing.

Finding strength spurred by adrenaline, she climbed upward, glancing back to see Eddy preparing himself for the jump.

Her legs pumped, pushed her up and over the wall of the open-topped car. The murderer made contact on the ladder below. She dropped into a cavity filled to the brim with wood chips and almost lost her balance on the uneven footing. Walking was difficult on a surface that kept shifting and threatening to suck her in like quicksand each time she took a step.

She'd struggled across only half the length of the car before she heard the "Oof!" that warned her Eddy was close behind.

She couldn't let him get his hands on her! Not again!

But, to her fury, Asia couldn't conceive of getting out alive and unscathed. Not when she had to reach the other end of the car, haul herself up to the rim, scoot over the side to the ladder and leap yet again before he caught up to her. Then she would have to cross the top of the boxcar that stood between her and the caboose.

Impossible, yet she didn't stop trying.

She was mere yards from her first goal when Eddy dived for her, tackling her bad leg.

"Aaahh!" Her scream echoed through the mountains.

Asia went down on her side, her fall softened by the padding of wood chips. Eddy was on his knees behind her, one hand hanging on to her ankle like a steel vise, the other caressing her calf.

And he was laughing, enjoying himself!

"What about it, baby doll? How about you and me finishing what we started on the beach?" he suggested in an oily voice. His fingers were climbing higher. "We got a nice bed and everything. Kind of like fate, huh? Only this time won't be for old Crawley. It'll be for me. For the trouble you put me through."

Asia saw red.

Every once of strength she possessed went into the kick she aimed at his grinning face. The flat of her foot made contact and jerked his head back as bright red spurted like a fountain from his nose. The second he loosened his grip, she pulled her other leg free.

"My nose! You broke it, you bitch!" His once-handsome face was contorted with fury and covered with blood.

He was gathering his strength.

She was getting to her feet.

The train lurched, sending them both off balance. Eddy fell forward, toward her, hands reaching. Panicked, Asia grabbed on to his hair and shoved him down face first. He howled in pain, and she kept the advantage. She leaped on his head with all her weight, sent it deeper into the shifting morass of wood chips while his arms flailed ineffectually.

Thinking of Marijo and the way he'd sent the redhead flying off the train, Asia wished he would smother, that he would choke to death very slowly and very painfully on the woody fiber. Then he couldn't hurt any woman, ever again.

But she didn't have what it took to kill another human being, no matter how much she wanted to, no matter how much Eddy Voss deserved death.

And, fearing he might somehow find the strength to throw her off him and thereby regain the advantage, she got to her feet and stomped hard on the back of his neck to stun him. Then she took off. Desperation giving wings to her feet over the unstable surface, Asia closed the few yards between her and the wall. She only hoped she'd bought herself enough time to get away from the bastard. She had no illusions about the painful revenge he'd wreak.

If he caught up to her...God help her, but she might be tempted to throw *herself* off the moving train.

"DOM, NO!" Jessica pleaded, her hands like claws on his arm as he tried to climb the platform railing. "You can't jump! You could fall on the tracks—you could be killed!"

Dominic hesitated for a moment, intent on making his sister understand his desperation. "You heard the scream, too, Jess. That had to be Asia. In my heart I know it. She needs me. I can't abandon her."

"Does she mean so much to you?"

"If something happens to her..." He let the sentence hang, didn't say that if Asia died, he'd have no reason to live. "Even if I wasn't in love with her, I would do this. Don't you understand? I owe it to her— *we* owe it to her. This may not be our fault, but it's because of us, and we're the only ones who can stop it."

He hardened himself to the stricken look on his sister's face. Jess had to understand. In the end she *had* to do the right thing, no matter how frightened she might be of going back. He saw no other way to stop his father's madness once and for all. Her wide green eyes glassed over with tears but she nodded and kissed his cheek.

"Be safe," she shouted above the clatter and clack of metal on metal.

Dominic gave her a quick squeeze and kiss in return.

Then he was off in a death-defying leap. The past two years of manual labor paid off in strength and steadiness. He easily met the boxcar's ladder and grabbed the rungs, the callused pads protecting his hands against all but the dullest pain. He found a footing and, after taking a second to get his wind, he was climbing to the top.

He was three-quarters of the way there when the train lurched as it took a hairpin curve. Dominic stayed put and clung to the metal wall. Waiting for the car to steady, he made the mistake of taking a quick look around.

On one side, the mountain.

On the other, a sheer drop, stunted and twisted trees clinging to the mountain's face the only thing between him and death.

His stomach lumped at the thought of such a horrible fate, but he put away his doubts and remembered Asia's beautiful face, her beautiful spirit. Even if he couldn't have her himself, he had to keep her safe!

He resumed his climb and had barely gotten to his feet on the roof when he saw a strand of blond hair fly over the opposite end of the boxcar.

"Asia?" he shouted against the wind. He moved forward carefully, keeping his legs spread for balance against the motion of the car. "Asia, are you all right?"

"Dominic?" She rose quickly, all the while looking down over her shoulder, unable to fight the hair that whipped across her face. "He's right behind me."

Then she was over the top on her hands and knees and Dominic met her. He stooped to help her up. Her eyes were wide, filled with fear. She was trembling and obviously fighting panic as she clutched at his arm and tried to drag him from the edge. He glanced over the end of the car to see Eddy Voss determinedly climbing the ladder.

"C'mon," he urged, now half carrying her as he crazily sped back toward the caboose.

He'd have time to give in to shock later. Eddy rather than Yerkes!

Another lurch sent them spilling toward the side of the car closest to the drop. Dominic stopped their momentum by purposely falling toward the car's center. Asia's feet slid close to the edge as he jerked her down next to him. He hung on to her wrist and she determinedly clambered back toward him. He glanced over his shoulder, saw Eddy, blood-smeared face filled with hatred and resolve, still clinging to the ladder.

Dominic knew then that both he and Asia weren't going to get off the boxcar before the killer caught up to them.

There was only one thing to do.

On his feet once more, he pulled her up, pushed her forward, forced her to the ladder.

"Dominic!" she protested, then looked behind him. Eyes wide, she moved fast.

At the end of the car, he motioned for her to descend first. He caught the doubt in her eyes before he turned to meet his enemy. Eddy was gaining on him at breakneck speed, a quarter of a car length away.

"Dominic, hurry!" Asia yelled, hesitating only a couple of rungs down.

Eddy slowed to grab something from his boot.

"Go!" Dominic demanded of Asia.

"Not without you!"

Words to warm his heart. But the next sound he heard was a sharp click that drowned out wheels and wind, echoed up the mountain and chilled his very soul.

"DOMINIC!" Asia screamed, mesmerized by the sight of the stiletto. "Please, come. We can get away from him!"

Fear welled in her for the man she loved. She yanked at the leg of his jeans, but he ignored her. Rather he moved forward, slightly crouching and ready for an attack.

"What's happening?" came a woman's shout from below.

Asia glanced down at a wide-eyed Jessica who stood on the platform of the caboose, thin hands gripping the rail. Asia didn't say anything, merely turned her back on Dominic's sister. She couldn't allay the frightened woman's fears. She was afraid, too, but she wasn't about to let someone die for her.

The two men were half-crouched and circling each other, getting closer to the center of the car and farther from her with each turn. Eddy was the only one armed. He jabbed the air, testing Dominic's mettle. Bile rose in her throat as Asia remembered the pain and fear caused by that very weapon.

The train swayed as the front half rounded a hairpin turn far ahead.

For a second, a light-headed Asia swayed, too, as she imagined herself on the hard-packed sand, Eddy's body pressing into her, pinning her with the tip of the blade. Then her vision cleared and she steadied herself as the men escalated their macabre dance.

Eddy lunged for real this time. Dominic buckled his body away from the blade.

"Why don't you stand still and meet your fate like a man?" the killer taunted, his flattened nose making him sound weird.

"Is that what you think you are, Eddy?" Dominic asked. "A real man? Hey, you're pretty good when you're up against a woman."

"Why, you—"

He lunged again. Dominic grabbed his arm and clung to it like a bulldog. Eddy brought his other fist around hard, catching Dominic in the side of the neck, making him let go instantly.

The thin blade swiped in an arch.

To Asia's horror, Dominic couldn't get out of the way fast enough. The honed metal glinted before embedding itself in his side. The train whistle shrilled as if signaling the victory. Blood splattered both men as Eddy whipped out the knife.

Asia screamed and scrambled back up the ladder. Focusing. Trying not to look down at the horrible, sickening drop into nothingness. She had to do something, to help the man she loved somehow, but he seemed so far away.

And she was impotent as Dominic staggered and Eddy slashed again, this time turning Dominic's arm red.

Even badly wounded, he had the presence of mind to yell, "Asia, get away!"

"Don't chase off the broad," Eddy chided in a mocking tone. "When I finish with you, I wanna have some *real* fun."

Dominic swung out ineffectually and Asia did the only thing she could think of to stop the maniac from killing him.

"He's King Crawley's son!" she yelled.

"Yeah, sure he is."

"If you kill him, Crawley will have you taken apart, a little at a time!"

"Nice try, but I'm not buying it."

The train whistled again, the sound a sharp warning against the mountain.

Asia ignored it.

Creating a distraction had bought Dominic a few precious seconds, some time to recover. He charged Eddy, forcing the man's knife arm away from his body long enough to shove the heel of his free hand into the killer's face.

Into his broken nose to be precise.

A new fountain of blood spurted forth, covering both men. Eddy screeched and dropped the knife, which went skittering off the side of the train. Rendered ineffectual, the killer sent both hands flying to his wounded face.

And then the boxcar completed the hairpin curve and Asia saw why the train's whistle had been warning them. Ahead loomed a wall of mountain. The front of the train had already been swallowed by a dark narrow oblong.

A tunnel!

"Dominic!" she cried. "Get down!"

But he was too busy trading punches with a stag-
gering Eddy to hear her…or to notice. The wood-chip
car was being swallowed by the mountain now.

"Dominic!"

When he continued to ignore her, continued to
punch an already senseless Eddy who somehow, by
some miracle, managed to stay on his feet, Asia leaped
on the man she loved and dragged him down.

"Aah!" he yelled in agony. "What did you do that
for?"

"The tunnel!"

Wide-eyed, Eddy turned to look as the stone arch
flew forward to meet him head-on with a sickening
smack. He went bouncing past Asia and Dominic and
tumbled off the train. Her ears rang with his scream,
which sounded endless as he dropped to certain death.

Lying there in the sudden dark, huddled against the
car roof, cheek vibrating against the metal, Asia
prayed there were no low spots in the tunnel. She could
almost feel the stone against her back now. Shaking
with relief, she thanked God she'd made it. And while
Dominic's breathing was shallow and ragged enough
to frighten her, he, too, was still alive.

She found out how much so a few minutes later
when the train cleared the tunnel. Dominic groaned to
a sitting position where he pulled her against his chest,
sticky and warm with the blood that covered him.

"My God, look what he did to you," Asia said,
afraid to let him press her too close.

"I'll live."

"You'd better," she said. "You'd better."

With a hand behind her head, Dominic pulled her
to him. Asia kissed the man she loved with passion

and gratitude, all the while trying not to hurt him any more than she had.

They would both live to see another day.

She only hoped it would be together.

HIS LEFT ARM AND SIDE sore and stiff, Dominic paced the dank little room and circled the table where his sister sat, nervously fidgeting with her hands.

While they waited for their father to be brought in, he replayed the past thirty hours in his head, starting with their arrival in Klamoth Bend to find George Yerkes waiting for them. He'd been afraid Yerkes had been in cahoots with Eddy, but he'd been dispelled of that notion immediately.

A Crawley household bodyguard at the time of her attack—the reason he'd been vaguely familiar to Dominic—Yerkes had held himself responsible for Jess's rape and subsequent disappearance. He'd overheard Asia and Dominic with his mother and had decided to follow them to the peninsula to see for himself if Jess was alive.

Yerkes seemed particularly fond of his sister . . . and to give the man credit, he'd been partly responsible for her being here now. Dominic sensed a bond that went beyond affection between the two that both disturbed and pleased him.

In Klamoth Bend, a doctor had seen to Dominic's wounds while a rescue team was dispatched. Eddy Voss had been found dead, his neck broken. A tree had prevented Marijo Lunt from going over the precipice. She'd survived with no more than a dislocated shoulder, a couple of fractured ribs and a mild concussion.

Dominic was saved from thinking about his separation from Asia too closely by the sound of footsteps in the hall. He retreated into a corner as the door opened.

"What is this?" came his father's voice. "I hate all this secrecy."

The graying, barrel-chested man who was his father entered and froze as his gaze lighted on Jessica. His eyes widened and he began trembling.

"Jess, am I seeing things, or is that you?"

She rose from the table and held out her arms. "Daddy."

King Crawley raced to her and gathered her close. "Jess, my sunshine. Where...how..."

It was the first time Dominic had ever heard his father at a loss for words.

"Dom convinced me to come back," Jessica said.

Crawley finally sensed his son's presence behind him. "Dominic!"

His face wreathed in a smile, he held out an expansive arm, but Dominic stayed where he was. The old man looked ill. Too thin. His skin a pasty gray. The disease had already ravaged him. He wanted to be embraced by his father's once-strong arm, but he couldn't move to him. Not yet. Maybe not ever unless King Crawley could forget who he was long enough to capitulate.

"Father."

Dominic nodded stiffly and remained in the corner. He was unable to miss his father's reaction. Hurt and something more. Could that be guilt?

"Daddy," Jess said, bringing the old man's attention back to her as she sat back down. "We have to talk."

"For as long as they'll let me." Crawley took the chair opposite. "We have so much to catch up on, starting with where you've been for almost two years."

Jessica took a deep breath. "Not about me. About the Rafertys."

Still behind his father, Dominic couldn't see the old man's expression. But his back went rigid.

"What about them?" he demanded.

"You have to stop this insane vendetta against them."

"I had perfectly good reasons—"

"Asia Raferty saved me from being raped if not killed," Jessica interrupted. "And she saved Dominic from certain death at the hands of Eddy Voss."

"Eddy? You mean Vinny," Crawley said. "A man of many aliases."

But Jessica was not to be distracted. "We owe Asia gratitude, not hatred."

But King Crawley seemed to be wound up in his own sick world. "An eye for an eye!" he said defensively. "My family was ruined. Judge Jasper Raferty was to blame."

"No, Daddy." Jessica looked to Dominic as if needing his strength. At his encouraging nod, she turned back to their father. "Put the blame where it belongs. *You,* not Judge Raferty, are responsible for what happened to me . . . for what happened to all of us."

"No!"

"Yes. You're the one who chose a life of crime. I wasn't raped because of who I was. I was raped because of who you were."

"Jess, baby, I'm so sorry about that."

Dominic was proud of his sister. He knew how difficult this was for her, but underneath the frail exterior, she was strong, a Crawley through and through.

"Are you really sorry?" she demanded. "Then prove it. Prove it, Daddy. Do this for me. Leave the Rafertys alone, please. They didn't deserve the hell you put them through. Enough."

Their father was silent for a moment, but his guilt hung heavy in the droop of his shoulders. He was a man who'd finally been defeated by life. Perhaps because he didn't want to be defeated by death also, Dominic thought, because he didn't want to die alone and suffer eternal damnation, the old man seemed to be relenting.

"Is that really what you want—"

"It is what I want," Jessica insisted. "And what Dominic wants."

His sister glared at him until Dominic came forward. Awkwardly he put a hand on the shoulder of the man he both loved and despised.

"If what I want matters to you after all these years," Dominic said.

King Crawley looked up at his son and Dominic realized his father really was a man defeated by his own crimes. His eyes were haunted.

"What you want has always mattered to me even if we didn't always agree, Dom." He patted the hand on his shoulder. "When I learned I was dying, I became desperate to prove I was still in control. I'll tell you something I never thought I'd admit. Revenge hasn't been all that sweet, and especially not when it endangered the people I loved. My children." A breath shuddered through him. "You're both alive. I'm thankful for that. But I'm ashamed you'll have to carry the scars of my making for the rest of your lives."

Knowing how difficult it was for his father to admit he was wrong, Dominic was moved. He squeezed his father's shoulder.

As King Crawley's gaze went from that of his daughter to his son, he made a solemn vow. "You have my word—the vendetta is ended."

ASIA WAS GOING to go nuts if she had to wait much longer. She was at the family home where the Raferty clan, except Jasper, gathered. Still in the hospital, their father was out of the cardiac intensive care unit and progressing nicely.

Why didn't Dominic call and tell her how the meeting with his father went?

"Hey, Asia." Dakota interrupted her silent reverie. "Syd read your tarot—you're going to have a long, happy life filled with a bunch of kids to keep you too busy to get into any more trouble."

At the mention of kids, he tugged a lock of baby-fine red hair. The little redhead on his lap smiled at him adoringly, as did Nora's mother, Honor, who moved closer to Dakota's side.

"He's got kids on the brain," Honor said, giving him a look that said she did, too.

"Great." Asia tried to make a joke of it. She spoke to Sydney who sat on the other side of the terrace table, shuffling her deck of tarot cards. "Did you happen to see who the father of my many children might be?"

"Well," her sister said, her expression teasing. "He's tall, dark and handsome."

Benno DeMartino strode through the double doors onto the terrace, the diamond stud in his ear winking as sunlight found it. "I'm already taken," he said. Joining Sydney, he bent to plant a long, lingering kiss on her lips. She flushed and looked prettier than Asia had ever seen her. Sydney was definitely a woman in love.

As was she, for all the good it did her!

Turning away from the cozy group at the table and strolling to the opposite end of the terrace, Asia fought her jealousy. She was happy for both of her siblings, of course, merely sad for herself. The day before, she and Dominic had parted like polite acquaintances.

And perhaps it was better that way, she told herself. Maybe they couldn't make it together. It would kill her to watch Dominic deny his needs and hide from who he was for the rest of his life.

As she stared up the hill toward the street, she spied a familiar tall, dark and handsome figure under a tree. He was leaning against the trunk, arms crossed over his chest, staring in her direction. How long had he been there?

"Dominic!"

Without a backward glance, Asia hopped over the cement fence and ran uphill to where he waited. She wanted to launch herself into his arms, but his expression stopped her. He'd closed himself off.

"What are you doing here?" she asked breath-
lessly, drinking in the sight of him. "Why didn't you
call?"

"I thought I should deliver the news in person.
You'll be happy to know my father ended the vendetta."

"Thank God," Asia said, her lids fluttering in relief.

Before she knew what he was about, Dominic
turned away from her and started to leave. Panicked,
she grabbed his arm and clung to him until he stopped
and faced her, his green eyes questioning.

"Do you love me?" she demanded to know.

He didn't say a word, but he couldn't hide the truth.
For once, she read him easily despite his effort to
cover. She launched herself against him. He
groaned—whether from physical or emotional pain—
and pushed her away.

Angrily, she shouted, "I love you, Dominic Crawford, and I don't intend to let you go."

He glowered at her. "What are you going to do to
stop me?"

"I've gotten pretty good at this detective business." She crossed her arms and lifted her chin. "If
you try to disappear on me, I'll follow you to the ends
of the earth. You know how pesty I can be."

"This won't work between us, Asia. I've told you
that before." But even as he protested, she noted the
spark of hope in his expression.

"It can work if we both want it badly enough!" she
insisted, her voice still raised. "I can't think of a man
more perfect for me."

"Perfect? I have nothing to offer you. No home, no career. I don't even have a simple job. I'd have to start over at something new. I wouldn't want to work in finance the way I did before. I think I only chose that route to prove something to my father."

A thrill shot through Asia. He was talking as if he wanted things to work between them. As if he were willing to pick up the pieces of his life and start again. No more running. No more hiding. That's what she'd been waiting to hear, what erased her last doubt.

"I'd stand by you," she promised. "You don't have to be a financial wizard. You can do anything that makes you happy."

"Asia," Dominic sighed as he took her into his arms. "Add persistent to the list."

But Asia wasn't thinking about lists as Dominic kissed her breathless. She wasn't thinking about anything but wanting him—until the noise of clapping and cheering got to her.

Turning in Dominic's arms, she smiled at the four adults and one little girl waving to them from the edge of the terrace. Their raised voices must have provided the others with entertainment.

"C'mon," Asia said, taking his hand and starting downhill. "It's time you met the rest of your future family."

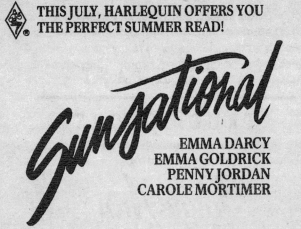

**This August, don't miss an exclusive
two-in-one collection of earlier love stories**

MAN
WITH A PAST

TRUE COLORS

**by one of today's hottest
romance authors,**

*Jayne Ann
Krentz*

Now, two of Jayne Ann Krentz's most loved books are
available together in this special edition that new and
longtime fans will want to add to their bookshelves.

Let Jayne Ann Krentz capture your hearts with the love
stories, MAN WITH A PAST and TRUE COLORS.

And in October, watch for the second two-in-one
collection by Barbara Delinsky!

Available wherever Harlequin books are sold.

HARLEQUIN
Romance®

**This August, travel to Spain
with the Harlequin Romance
FIRST CLASS title #3143,
SUMMER'S PRIDE
by Angela Wells.**

"There was a time when I would have given you everything I
possessed for the pleasure of taking you to my bed and loving
you...."

But since then, Merle's life had been turned upside down, and
now it was clear that cynical, handsome Rico de Montilla felt
only contempt toward her. So it was unfortunate that when she
returned to Spain circumstances forced her to seek his help.
How could she hope to convince him that she was not the
mercenary, unfeeling woman he believed her to be?

Back by Popular Demand

A romantic tour of America through fifty favorite Harlequin Presents, each set in a different state researched by Janet and her husband, Bill. A journey of a lifetime in one cherished collection.

In August, don't miss the exciting states featured in:

Title #13 — ILLINOIS
         The Lyon's Share

#14 — INDIANA
         The Indy Man

Available wherever
Harlequin books are sold.

Take 4 bestselling love stories FREE

Plus get a FREE surprise gift!

Special Limited-time Offer

Mail to
Harlequin Reader Service®
3010 Walden Avenue
P.O. Box 1867
Buffalo, N.Y. 14269-1867

YES! Please send me 4 free Harlequin Intrigue® novels and my free surprise gift. Then send me 4 brand-new novels every other month, which I will receive months before they appear in bookstores. Bill me at the low price of $2.47 each—a savings of 28¢ apiece off cover prices. There are no shipping, handling or other hidden costs. I understand that accepting the books and gift places me under no obligation ever to buy any books. I can always return a shipment and cancel at any time. Even if I never buy another book from Harlequin, the 4 free books and the surprise gift are mine to keep forever.

180 BPA AC9H

Name	(PLEASE PRINT)
Address	Apt. No.
City	State	Zip

This offer is limited to one order per household and not valid to present Harlequin Intrigue® subscribers. Terms and prices are subject to change. Sales tax applicable in N.Y.

INT-BPA2DR   © 1990 Harlequin Enterprises Limited

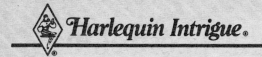
Harlequin Intrigue ®

QUID PRO QUO

You have just read the exciting conclusion to Patricia Rosemoor's
QUID PRO QUO trilogy. Dominic and Asia, two people willing to risk
their lives in order to end a madman's quest for vengeance, conquer
the odds and find the true meaning of love.

Now you have the opportunity to read the book that introduces the
series. Meet Sydney Raferty in #161 PUSHED TO THE LIMIT. Driven
to the brink of insanity, Sydney must find her way back to reality....
Then continue the adventure with Dakota Raferty, the judge's only
son, who finds himself in a race against time as he tries to save a
little girl's life in #163 SQUARING ACCOUNTS.

Read all the books in Patricia Rosemoor's QUID PRO QUO trilogy.
